MANSOUR'S
EYES

MANSOUR'S EYES

Ryad Girod

Translated from the French by
Chris Clarke

**TRANSIT
BOOKS**

Published by Transit Books
2301 Telegraph Avenue, Oakland, California 94612
www.transitbooks.org

Les Yeux de Mansour © P.O.L Editeur, 2019
English translation copyright © Chris Clarke 2020

ISBN: 978-1-945492-36-5 (paperback)
LIBRARY OF CONGRESS CONTROL NUMBER: 2020937464

DESIGN & TYPESETTING
Justin Carder

DISTRIBUTED BY
Consortium Book Sales & Distribution
(800) 283-3572 | cbsd.com

Printed in the United States of America

9 8 7 6 5 4 3 2 1

إلهي هدأت الأصوات وسكنت الحركات،
وخلا كل حبيب بحبيبه،
وقد خلوت بك أيها المحبوب،
فاجعل خلوتي منك في هذه الليلة عتقي من النار.

My God, now that the voices have been
appeased and all has grown calm
Now that each lover has retired with their beloved
I retire with You, O My Beloved.
Let this retreat, during this night, be for me
deliverance from the fire.

Rabiʿah al-ʿAdawiyya

1.

We wait. All of Riyadh seems to be waiting. Soon it will be 10 a.m. and Al Safat Square is already dark with people. It shouldn't be long now. All the nearby businesses have closed and the streets are filling up in the wake of a white 4x4, its speakers blasting the announcement of a heretic's execution after Friday prayers. Everyone has gathered in Justice Square, where society puts its sinners to death. We wait. It's hot, already very hot, and the sun cruelly floods the scene. A sandstorm has blown all night long, leaving behind, as if in suspension, a dust that seems to multiply the light's brilliance. The sky is white. We form a more and more compact crowd around a pail of water and some rags that the courthouse's employees have placed at the point they reckoned to be the exact center, the true middle of this large square typically occupied by women and children. This morning, there are only men, and real men, necessarily. In a few minutes' time, the blade of a saber will slice through the neck of a body that will be divided into two parts. It takes a man to watch that. It's nearly 10 a.m. and I leave the square to make my way back across the three hundred yards separating it from the courthouse, out of which will come Mansour al-Jazaïri, my friend. Policemen cleave the crowd in half, forming a cordon to expand the circle that surrounds the pail of water and the rags. One of them unrolls a rug, or rather a mat, just big enough to hold the two separated parts. The tension mounts, the impatience, and the fear as well. The cell phones are out, some are already starting to film and we can already hear, from here and there in the crowd, *Gassouh! Gassouh!* Cut it off! Cut it off! With difficulty, I again cross the three hundred yards packed with Arabs, Afghans, Asians, all mingling together for the occasion along this road down which Mansour will have to make his way so that he can kneel, lower his head, stick out his neck, and free himself from his transgression. Purify himself. *Gassouh! Gassouh!* Policemen are now positioning themselves in front of the great door of the tribunal. It shouldn't be long now.

You see, Mansour had told me, it's like making love without coming. An empty and hopeless undertaking . . . Months of saving up to buy myself this car and now nothing . . . there's nothing more to it, I have it, end of story. Nothing more to it! The entire time we sat there talking, he continued to interject that Nothing!, shooting a sorrowful look over our surroundings as we sat drinking coffee at a table at the Starbucks located in the Royal Mall. This despite the fact that we had come here to celebrate the purchase he had just made, his acquisition of a beautiful red 6.2L Camaro V8 capable of going from zero to a hundred and sixty miles per hour in under fifteen seconds. Nothing, he said. Whereas for me, excited as a child, impatient to hear the roar of the engine, impatient to feel my stomach clench from the acceleration, I was squirming with impatience in front of the mug I had quickly drained so as to be ready to climb into the leather interior of that sports model and I was . . . jealous, yes, jealous, terribly jealous, but at the same time happy for my friend Mansour, absent before his own coffee, his gaze blank. Mansour, paralyzed where he sat, as if melted, folded in on himself and extraneous to all the agitation that reigned over this mall full of people coming and going, their arms loaded with all sorts of bags . . . single people, people in groups, people with their families, from store to store . . . as if the entire city had gathered here, in this mall, to live here. People coming and going and crossing paths, and yet all seemingly going in the same direction, following the same path, heading for the same fate . . . until our eyes landed on a father and his daughter. They walked right in front us, and shot us a look that was both surprised and curious . . . which they then diverted from us, almost simultaneously, to calmly continue on their way to the central roundabout of the Royal Mall. Spanish, or French, I had thought as I continued to observe the father, one hand holding onto his daughter, three or four years old, and the other a dozen bags. Mansour followed the pair with me as they skirted the crowd on their way to the first free bench, where the father set down his bags and released his daughter's hand; she immediately went to place her feet within the large black circle that demarcated the central roundabout of the Royal Mall . . . to then run in a circle and laugh herself silly. Maybe to counter the force of inertia that was drawing her toward the middle, or maybe simply for fun, the little girl swung her arms like a propeller . . . which had the effect of multiplying her laughter and drawing the attention of other children. As for her father, he stared off into space waiting for the game to come to an end or for his wife to return from the shops that had detained her or quite

simply for things to happen as they do, just like that, with time
working its magic, and upon each lap made by his daughter, he
perfunctorily shot out a Take it easy, Azadeh! . . . or Aziadeh . . .
to which, each time, the marvelous little girl replied, in French,
Oui papa! So maybe they were French but originally from Iran
or Turkey . . . or Iranians who speak French . . . who is to
say? Then a Starbucks employee brought us back to reality by
collecting our coffee cups, which he decided were empty, giving the table a quick wipe with a rag soaked with antibacterial
cleaner. Damp streaks traced across the surface each time only
to disappear almost instantly, giving the glass that covered the
table a somewhat lackluster look. When we turned back to the
father and his marvelous little girl, all we saw was a newly liberated bench and a central roundabout crisscrossed by women
dressed all in black. They had left, it was as if they had disappeared. This whole time, Mansour had maintained his stony
look, which he suddenly decided to break, saying to me: It's as
if they never existed.

As he got to his feet, Mansour was overcome by a violent
headache that forced him to remain still and hold onto my arm.
Upright, he looked in the direction of the central roundabout,
raised his hands to clutch his head, and told me: My head hurts . . . you
know, I've been getting headaches more and more often lately . . .
He explained to me that recently, they hadn't been letting up,
the pain came more and more frequently, sharper and sharper,
and it even woke him up in the middle of the night and the
usual pills didn't really do anything to help, that he really ought
to see a doctor soon. More and more people were circulating
within the mall's galleries, balmy with the fragrance of oud, a
scent that rose up from the immaculate tiles and clung to the
glittering shop windows. Galleries that we hastily followed in

search of an exit and fresh air, in the hope that Mansour's pain would subside. In the parking lot, my friend still had that blank stare as he looked at his beautiful red Camaro, and admitted that he was still suffering. You drive, he instructed me, holding out the keys . . . I didn't need to be asked twice, and quickly set off. The hum of the engine seemed to reach all the way to my heart, but the traffic along Takhassusi dampened my excitement. I moved forward frustratingly, in little bursts, making do with short accelerations. Endlessly running into red lights the length of the avenue. Get us out of here, he demanded. Into the desert. As soon as I was able, I took Mekkah Road and let the engine loose like I was freeing a wild animal. I shouted to him, Due west, with the sun right in our faces! as if I was inquiring about his state. That'll be fine . . . he replied with a smile. And it's true that it was fine. At that time of day, the sunset hour, the sky offered us a spectacular show. A silence came over us in the leather-clad cockpit of the Camaro, we could barely hear the rumble of its belly or the wind that whistled by at our passage, a silence within which we gazed upon the succession of boulders, gilt by the radiance of the sun, as they flew past us at full speed. The immense rocky plateau was cleaved in two by Mekkah Road; it was deserted, magnificent, giving way to sheer cliffs that looked out over a long expanse of red dunes we could make out, at that moment, only intermittently, at the end of each *wadi* or the bottom of each dizzying crevasse over which bridges gave the impression that they were trying to stitch together, bring closer, connect every escarpment on the plateau. The Camaro's windshield became a movie screen in front of our eyes as it received the gentle orange light of a setting sun, hanging there, applying itself like a cream, a golden film across Mansour's face as he stared straight ahead. Without

blinking. Receiving upon his eyes the burning attention of the
star toward which we were heading. Strangely, that sun in my
eyes feels really good, he told me . . . I hardly feel the pain anymore. The entire leather interior of the beautiful Camaro was
bathed in a sort of golden cloud, saffron-colored, and the gentle
suspension, likely hydraulic, gave me the feeling I was floating
or levitating above the rocky plateau . . . flying across a velvety
smoothness that covered the stony expanse. At this hour, the
desert offered a spectacular show. You know, he said, I often have
this strange dream where I find myself all alone in a prairie. A sad,
yellowish prairie, where I'm walking with no real destination,
where I continue on without really knowing where I'm going.
The grass is tall, dry, and I can hear it brushing against my legs.
And I can smell it. I keep going, I keep going, until I see, each
time, in what seems to me to be the very middle of that prairie,
an animal lying there. I move toward it, it's an ass. A beige donkey,
or rather, light brown, an ass lying on his flank, his hooves splayed
out, his head stretched out over that dry grass and his eyes wide
open. He isn't dead, no, but he isn't sleeping, either, he's just lying
there and I get the feeling that he's waiting for me. I look at him,
I look at his beige coat, or rather, his brown one, and I instantly
feel calm. I approach him, he doesn't react . . . I sit down, right
up against him, still he doesn't react. I feel calm, I feel content, I
reach out my hand, I bring it to him, I feel his coarse hair, I sink
my fingers into it, I stroke it. This dream always seems to last all
night . . . Snuggled up against an ass all night, can you imagine? . . .
Right then the road began to plummet dizzyingly between two
cliffsides. We left the plateau of the Najd and Mansour reverted
to silence. The dunes, red, infinite, received us.

   Gassouh! Gassouh! They're yelling now, brandishing their
cell phones toward the door of the tribunal, a heavy door, as

if embedded or even brazed into the outer wall. And people continue to converge. The crowd invites more crowd. Hatred, curiosity, fear, boredom, conviction, misunderstanding, expectation, vengeance . . .

I brought the beautiful red Camaro to a stop on a little road, gnawed by sand in spots, bordering the dunes. The sun continued its flamboyant descent as Mansour opened his door, climbed out without closing it behind him, and then advanced toward the mineral immensity that undulated all around us. Ignorance, severity, compassion, love, mercy, violence . . . His footsteps sank lightly into sand I imagined to be cool, from the leather interior where I had remained to roll a joint, following him with my eyes as he sunk down into the hollow between two dunes, then climbed the slope, responding to what seemed to be a summons . . . Piety, impiety, madness, wisdom . . . He reached the crest and followed its line as would a tightrope walker until he found the point he judged best to stop, to sit and contemplate . . . or perhaps he had stopped just like that, by chance, without any real reason, feeling the place sufficiently high up that he might contemplate the interminable expanse of the dunes or the rocky pediment by way of which we had come . . . or perhaps he was contemplating, further down from where we were by then standing side by side, the vast surface of the sand, which formed a sort of basin, like a dish, fully rounded, which I then saw as a small prairie of dry, yellow grass, in which I sought out an ass amid the grains of sand . . . while he, Mansour, was simply looking at the billions upon billions of grains . . . You'll end up getting your head chopped off if you keep smoking that shit, my friend had warned me, with an evident lack of clairvoyance and intuition . . . or maybe it was a slightly erroneous premonition? A simple error in discernment?

But we weren't there yet in that moment . . . Atop the rocky pediment that proudly towered across from us, the shadows of the dunes chipped away at the sunshine that remained on that dry and dusty land. It was time for us to go. Mansour was feeling better. As for me, I felt my eyes burning in the dry air and saw the dunes dance in the growing dimness . . . I got into the passenger seat and looked, through the window, at the earth as it continued to shift, stretching off into the distance. More or less lying down in my seat, my head resting against the leather of the door, I checked in and out at the whim of my states of consciousness and unconsciousness, I let myself drift away. In the distance, like the lights of a beacon, the twinkling of Kingdom Tower drew the beautiful red Camaro toward it as we sailed through the desert.

Gassouh! Gassouh! shouts the crowd when the heavy door of the tribunal opens and two men step out. They advance toward the onlookers, requesting they back away with sweeping gestures, stretching out their arms and waving their hands without the slightest trace of ambiguity. It's clear now, we can hear them, they ask everyone to back up. Violently. *Gassouh! Gassouh!* responds the crowd, and the two men go back the way they came. The seconds drag on, interminable. The silence folds in on itself like a promise that has worn thin and then been recanted. The seconds drag on, intolerable, and the two men reappear, followed by two policemen flanking Mansour, his head bowed and buried in the large folds of a white turban. We cannot see his face . . . only his hands and feet, bare, at the extremities of a long white tunic. Dirty. His hands and feet hobbled by a thick chain . . . his hands and feet shackled and linked by a heavy chain, which forces him to hunch and to stumble. And behind Mansour, one last man, large and strong, wearing a black cape embroidered in gold and firmly holding a long saber and a Qur'an . . . *Gassouh! Gassouh!* cries the crowd once again, despite the evidence that things are in place and inevitably moving forward. And those billions of particles of dust, in suspension, hesitating to fall, smaller even than particles: molecules, atoms, those billions upon billions of dust atoms in suspension, multiplying the lackluster whiteness of the morning, aggregating to form a sort of whitish fog, thick, compact, and seeming to freeze not only the space but also the time around this scene in which Mansour comes to a halt, then raises his head then looks at us before resuming his march. Looks at us, all of us. A scene frozen like an old snapshot.

Perhaps Abdelkader, smack dab in the middle of the nineteenth century, had worn the same look when he was asked to pose for that photograph, when he was taken from the room in which he had been sequestered, when he was brought outside for better lighting, outside of what seemed more hovel than castle, and was asked to put on his handsome white burnoose, for prestige, asked to stand atop a beam of sorts that raised him up a few inches so that he would be perfectly inset within the frame of one of the hidden doorways of what seemed more Prison de France than Château d'Amboise, so that the shot would be a good one, and when they asked him to pose and when he tried to find a gaze that might correspond to what was expected of him, or perhaps he didn't have to seek one out, maybe he simply balanced himself on that beam of sorts, which acted as a display stand, and waited until the photographer had finished his work, listening to the Loire flowing by further down, and perhaps thinking, as he did each day, each hour, and each minute, of the words of the Duke of Aumale, or perhaps those of General de Lamorcière, of the promise given, mulled over each day and each hour and each minute of his imprisonment by the banks of the Loire, along with his entire tribe, his entire *smala* as they said in those days, the duke's word specifying a safe house and protection in Alexandria or in Akka, and he, the old emir, not being able to comprehend such a betrayal, a breach of the promise made, waiting patiently for the error to be corrected, the misunderstanding . . . waiting through interminable seconds for this liberation that must surely take place . . . because a nobleman, a descendant of the king, could not go back on his word, the word of France. Or maybe that look had been the one he was already wearing, ashamed and humiliated at having led his entire *smala* and perhaps an entire nation to cold and to death, or perhaps he was worried about what he had dared write to the royalty: *If you were to bring me, on behalf of your king, all the wealth of France, in millions and in diamonds, and if it were possible for me to hold it all in the flaps of this burnoose, I would sooner hurl it into the waters that lap against the walls of my prison than release you from the oath you have solemnly sworn to me. I will carry this promise within me until the grave. I am your guest. Make of me your prisoner if you so desire, but the shame and dishonor will weigh upon you and not me.* Whatever it was, he did not have to seek very far to find a suitable look, he just had to maintain the one he had worn since he had been taken there, he and his entire *smala*, to that damp and cold land where the Loire flowed shallow and slow. The strange gaze that he brought to bear upon that world, which must have been the absolute inverse, or the exact opposite, of his own world. Today, Mansour is looking at us with what is undoubtedly that same strangeness. His eyes are clear. My God how they are clear! Pale eyes, as if made of glazed earthenware, which pan across this unrelenting crowd, as if he meant to look at each one of us. Then he lowers those oddly pale eyes, seems to look at the ground, and resumes his march forward. *Gassouh! Gassouh!*

2.

SEATED ON ONE OF THE BENCHES in the long corridor that served
as a waiting room for the neurology department of Kingdom
Hospital, I was waiting for Mansour, looking distractedly at the
comings and goings of the Filipino nurses who enlivened their
every passing with a Good morning Sir! in English that was
intended for me, or intended for one of the three other patients
dispersed along the long corridor, or intended for the walls
or for the tiling, seeing as they were never looking at anyone
in particular before they dashed into one of the six examination rooms to drop off folders or pick them up. Over the past
few days, the pain had intensified to the point that it prevented
Mansour from sleeping or working, and also from having
another encounter with his donkey, I thought with a smile,
catching the eye of another nurse. Good morning Sir! For what
had now been nearly an hour, behind the door across from me,
Mansour had been explaining his situation, his sharp pains, his
slowed speech, maybe even his donkey . . . to the doctor I had

caught a glimpse of and who hadn't seemed all that sharp, all that responsive, when he had seen Mansour holding his head in his hands and had asked him if he was ill . . . But perhaps I was mistaken, who is to say?

Gassouh! Gassouh! continue the cries coming from among the many eyes that watch Mansour al-Jazaïri pass by, the opposite of what the crowd must have been like when it gathered along the edges of the principal artery of Damascus, in 1965, during the passage of that coffin covered by the Syrian flag and containing the remains, or rather what remained of the remains, which is to say ashes or even less, the totality wrapped in a shroud and spread across the bottom of that coffin taken from the Muhyi al-Din Mosque in Salihiyya to be set on a sort of chariot and paraded before the reddened eyes of the military, the high dignitaries and common citizens, all of them sincerely moved by what remained of the remains of Abdelkader al-Jazaïri as they passed by, draped in the nation's colors. Eyes reddened because, for each one of them, these were not remains or ashes, but Abdelkader himself, resting intact within that coffin the Syrian nation was to send to the Algerian nation. To send as if to send back, to repay a debt, a full century later, to return to the Algerian state the founder of the State itself. And a few hours later, which is to say a few thousand miles away, to the west, the welcome on the tarmac of Algiers Airport, to the sound of canons firing, of this same coffin, removed from the belly of the plane and covered, this time, with the Algerian flag. And the president, in person, approaching the casket alongside the members of his government so as to lift it up on their shoulders and advance toward the platform decorated with flowers and flags the color of the recently and at-long-last independent State . . . to set the Emir Abdelkader down upon it and stand at attention, to pass in review the different corps of that young army as it marched to the rhythm of the new national anthem, halting, swift, curt, firm, hands just as firmly held to foreheads, and heads turned toward the emir for a first and final military salute. Soldiers marching, their bodies rigid, their movements self-assured, chins held aloft and eyes not reddened this time, but instead vague, or, to put it another way, their gazes were nothing less than undecided and circumspect . . . And the president himself, his eyes like this as well, pondering perhaps the complexity of the task, wondering where to begin, as if already exhausted by the very scale of the mission to be carried out, namely that of constructing, crafting, carving from all these distinct pieces a myth, a hero, a symbol, a martyr for a grateful homeland . . . or perhaps not, having those same eyes only because the matter was already underway and would take care of itself. Eyes of boredom, then, idleness and laziness, because soon there would be nothing left to do, no headstones to be put in place, nor even epitaphs to be engraved, no heavy bronze statues to be erected that would fix in time, and in space, for that matter, a horse rearing up on its hind legs, mounted by what had ceased to be a pile of ashes only to be remade into a fiery horseman brandishing a menacing saber . . . and whether or not he considered this magnificent bearded man he saw lying peacefully before him, through the flag, through the oak, to be a traitor or a renegade, and even if he might have preferred to spit on him instead of honor him . . . even if this were the case, he impassibly maintained this vague gaze that seemed to be waiting for things to happen as they do . . . who is to say?

Good morning Sir! Then the nurse disappeared behind the door across from me, allowing me only a fraction of a second in which to see Mansour, listless, his arms hanging limply down the side of the chair he sat in as he listened to the voice, a voice that reached me for a fraction of a second as well, or rather I struggled to hear and understand that voice expressing itself half in Arabic, half in English, trying its best to explain where things stood. And then, a few minutes later, the door opened with the nurse once again holding the knob and this time the doctor holding Mansour's arm as if to gently push him out of the examination room . . . and then, imperceptibly, suddenly, all four of us there in front of the already-closed door, the nurse still holding its knob and the doctor addressing me, asking me if I was a relative of Mansour's, to which I responded that sort of, yes, seeing as we had known each other ever since French high school in Damascus and we had come from Syria together and we had worked for the same company for a decade . . . So, how else to put it . . . he explained to me that Mansour would need to be taken care of, that it was a rare disease, an orphan disease, degenerative . . . that in a manner of speaking, the impulses of the nervous system, or electrical, he had said, had reversed themselves . . . and in some way, the cells, or the gray matter, he had called it, instead of developing, was retracting, becoming condensed, and would end up dying off . . . it was this reversal in the direction of cerebral activity that was producing the pain, because the system wasn't used to it, and these pains would fade and then disappear . . . However, Mansour was going to progressively become an idiot, he was going to lose all intelligence, the doctor had told me . . . that at first it wouldn't be visible but that it was necessary to be vigilant, he had insisted . . . Hold his hand when you cross the street, Dr. Maarafi had concluded, shooting us both a large smile to confirm that, in some way, this was intended to be funny . . . but not that funny. All of this despite the fact that two hours earlier we had been in a completely different reality, one that had become forever inaccessible after what the doctor had just said . . . two hours earlier, Mansour had woken up, he had showered and shaved, had drunk his coffee and swallowed two painkillers, looking out the bay window as the sun rose over Riyadh . . . then, just like every morning of every week, he had opened his armoire and pulled on a shirt, a suit and a tie . . . then he had made his way to the bathroom to spritz his neck and hands with a scent that he paid a fortune for when he managed to get over to Muscat. A subtle mélange of oud and sandalwood that an artisan perfumer knew just how to dose out in order to magnify their essences, because, for Mansour, a person's scent was what distinguished them, what defined them, and it was important to him that his own be appropriately subtle. And yet right then, facing the doctor who maintained his smile, despite the scent of oud and sandalwood, despite the suit and tie, the dangling arms and the impassivity of his face . . . there was no longer anything subtle about Mansour. Just the opposite. A clown, I had secretly thought, a grotesque clown. And I really thought I had let out a cry, although I may have only done it mentally, in any case I had cried out in my head: No! No! Don't say that! when the doctor had specified that it was irreversible.

Gassouh! Gassouh! shouts the crowd at the sight of what is perhaps no longer anything more than a vegetable, advancing as might a beast of burden, a cow, an ass . . . a body depleted of its spirit . . . just a collection of organic matter, of living matter, which the stroke of a saber will divide in two, transforming it into two masses of dead matter much like the wave of a magic wand . . . perhaps Mansour is no longer any more than that, any more than meat . . . who is to say what remains of Mansour within Mansour's head?

The way I remember it, the corridors of the neurology department had abruptly grown dark, like it was the middle of the night when we took our leave first of the doctor and then of his nurse, who had insisted on accompanying us all the way to the elevator door only to disappear again just as quickly, back into that corridor still plunged into darkness, the echo of a warm and hospitable Goodbye Sir! trailing behind her . . . Mansour remained mute during the time it took us to leave the hospital and make our way back to the Camaro. I didn't dare say a thing, didn't even dare look at him, picturing his blank and immobile gaze . . . and turning over and over in my mind everything the doctor had said. I started the engine and drove through a city that I no longer even saw . . . without a goal, without a specific destination, I drove down anything that presented itself before me . . . avenues, roads, lanes, highways and byways, we just kept going. And I rummaged around in Mansour's head, I tried to imagine the disorder of the cells in that enormous web, spun throughout a lifetime and abruptly jumbled by the reversal of electrical or nervous impulses . . . and for what reason? There's what the doctor hadn't specified, the reason. A virus? A congenital defect? A genetic predisposition? Or was it simply chance? Just like that, without any reason whatsoever, the nervous impulses had begun to slow down on their way through the tissues, the canals, had then frozen for an instant, a second or a fraction of a second during which Mansour would have felt a violent shock and then they would have set off in the opposite direction, just like that, completely by chance . . . a current moving against the tide, traveling through panicked membranes, just like that, without any reason, because of some inescapable and merciless whim of providence . . . It had come over Mansour just like that, perhaps while he meandered peacefully through the mall's galleries, balmy with the fragrance of oud . . . Was it an indirect and adverse effect of the oud? Was it due to an excess of oud? And yet, a surplus of oud leads to harmony, the saying goes . . . but still . . . While he meandered peacefully past the glittering shop windows of the Royal Mall, lusting after the many items on their display stands, the short-circuit, in a manner of speaking, had beset him, forcing him to stop, to stand frozen in place, perhaps to the laughter of children or even the laughter of women. And he had held his head for fear it would explode, had looked straight ahead, his eyes fixed on something, little matter what it was, something tangible and fixed and concrete and real like a sign on the wall an extinguisher a bench, little matter, something from that reality to which he could cling so as not to be carried away by the violence of the pain . . . Or perhaps it had been elsewhere, before the yellow of the desert or the red of the dunes, while he contemplated in solitude the billions upon billions of grains of sand, that fate had struck its blow . . . as he faced that nature, which to him seemed fixed, relaxing in communion with that nature, calm and gentle, the thunderbolt of providence had flashed down to strike him. Unjustly, as only providence knows how . . . Before those billions upon billions of grains of sand, a bolt of lightning had passed through him, yanking a cry from his throat, throwing back his head, inside of which thousands of electrocuted, fried neurons had been transformed into common grains of sand . . . and, as he came back to his senses, in the shrill echo of his cry, he raised his eyes skyward as if to make out where the bolt had come from.

And so, still inside the muffled silence of the Camaro's leather interior, I didn't have it in me to turn toward Mansour. I only imagined him, from what little passed within my field of

vision, sitting there like a statue, a mannequin of hardened plas-
tic, and then guessed what he was holding in his hands once he
had fumbled through the inner pocket of his suit and unfolded
his wallet . . . I knew that in his hands, he held a photo that
had been passed down to him by his father or his grandfather,
a photo he carried around religiously, a photo worn scratched
and streaked by time and by fingers but that bore witness, like
an ID card, to his filiation. Abdelkader's face, in black and
white, the black having turned to gray and the white more
yellowish, the size of a passport photo, which had eluded the
emir's iconography archives to make its way into the pockets of
his great-great-grandchild who held it, during that moment, in
the palm of his hand. At the edge of my field of vision, I saw
his lips move and I eventually heard him muttering under his
breath, something that I could still make out seeing as I already
knew what it was he said, this recitation, for having heard it a
thousand times, as he listed off names like the beads of a rosary
so as not to forget them and to transmit them from generation
to generation . . . ascending, Mansour bin Soltane bin Hassan
bin Mohamed bin Abdelkader bin Muhyi al-Din bin Mustafa
. . . bin Hasan bin Fatimah bint Muhammad, may peace and
salvation be upon him . . . and descending, from the Prophet
Muhammad abu Fatimah umm Hasan bin ʿAli, then Hasan abu
Hasan al-Muthana abu ʿAbd Allah al-Kamil abu Idris al-Awwal
. . . abu Muhyi al-Din abu Abdelkader abu Mohamed abu
Hassan abu Soltane abu Mansour al-Jazaïri . . . in a loop, as we
drove around Riyadh not knowing where we should stop. In a
loop, a tête-à-tête, face to face and eye to eye with his ancestor
and maybe with that same gaze . . . shared between the two of
them. Empty at first glance and, even when looking at it head
on, always giving the impression that it's aimed slightly off to

the side . . . as if it were seeing something else. Eventually, by weaving our way through the teeming city, we just happened to arrive at his place, without really knowing how. I accompanied him, silently, withdrawn, into his apartment. Without saying anything to me, Mansour made his way to the bathroom. There he took refuge, locked himself away. I could smell the scent of oud incense, persistent, it seemed to float in the air, and on the orange light that the blinds let into the living room. Stifled sobs reached me and chilled me to the bone. Pain. Embarrassment. Helplessness. I set the keys to the Camaro down on the table by the entrance and closed the door behind me.

Gassouh! Gassouh! they cry, whereas only three months earlier, Mansour and I had instead heard Good morning Sir! Goodbye Sir! in the corridors of the neurology department of Kingdom Hospital. And then the diagnosis, the illness, like a cancer that was to carry him off in three months' time. Does he even hear? Does he even understand? I don't know. I watch and I listen to it all as if it lacks in consistency, like a feeling of lightness . . . I weigh the insignificance of things, the insignificance of everything, as simple as a Good morning Sir! Goodbye Sir! Mansour advances, his body in chains, and perhaps he's feeling this way as well . . . he continues forward, following a trajectory straight toward what must be the very center of the square, where a rag and a pail await him . . . next to which he will kneel and stick out his neck to welcome the blade that will calm the clamor of the crowd. All these people who cannot accept that a Muslim, like them, that an Arab, like them, could utter . . . the unutterable, they think, as giant, as thundering, and as simple as *I am Him.* As if no person, no *I,* could purify himself, simplify himself, reduce himself, lighten himself, and raise himself up as far as *Him.* Let alone an Arab. As if nothing so great could ever, nor should ever, come from an Arab. Apart from the Prophet, the rest of them should remain nothing more than depraved Bedouins, boors, without culture and without grandeur. Too dirty and too impious to approach Him and love Him . . . they should endure the contempt and the severity of an intransigent and distant creator . . . should reconcile themselves, until the end of their days, to a resounding no. Any prayers, any reverence, would have to go unheeded among the sterile and dry sands of Arabia, of the Orient . . .

Just like how a century and a half earlier, the French dignitaries had met the emir's complaints with the same contempt and, perhaps worse than contempt, indifference . . . reading those letters in Emir Abdelkader's own hand, perhaps amazed by their style or maybe not even noticing it, Lamoricière, or some other representative of the French Republic, put the letters back exactly where he had found them and asked his secretary to reply to them, to reply in the customary way, then he returned to those close to him, which is to say to his family, or maybe his friends, or maybe other generals, to concern himself with the expansion of France, with working to cultivate the grandeur of France, leaving it to his aide-de-camp to grant a minute or two to this Bedouin who, strangely, he may have thought, preferred the emptiness of the desert to castle life . . . And so, with those eyes of his, standing on that beam of sorts to frame the locale they had washed up in, he and his people, in the depths of that eternally damp Indre-et-Loire, with that gaze fixed by the click of the photographer, a look that one might read as making plain as day the utter renunciation, the absolute apathy, the irreversible dehumanization . . . even a congenital idiocy . . . that gaze having ended, perhaps a few hours after the departure of the photographer and the officials from the newly established French Republic, he set to inscribing words of a prophetic subtlety to express his indignation: *My aged mother and the women of my household cry night and day, and no longer give any credibility to the hope that I have been obliged to offer them right up until the end. What am I saying? Not only the women, but the men, too, have succumbed to lamentations. Their state is such that I am persuaded, should our captivity be prolonged much longer, that many shall die of it. And it is I who was the cause of all of this misery! It was I alone who had intended to give myself over to them! Is there not in France a tribunal charged with hearing the grievances and complaints of the victims of injustice? With this Republic, you have achieved a great work which promises to spread good fortune upon all. Make certain that I am not an exception.*

I seek out Mansour's eyes from within this crowd that roils like a turbulent river, which I attempt to make my way back up, against the current . . . I pass one shoulder and then another, one head and then another, only to find myself the same distance away from my friend. I seek his eyes as if they had the power to pull me out of there. I seek his eyes because they have the power to reduce distances in the same way as when I was laboriously climbing the dune where he, Mansour, still rested, sitting lightly, and, while I continued to toil away, to sink into the goldenness of the sand, he offered up his eyes to me. Luminous. While I struggled for breath and tried to attract his attention, he turned his gaze on me like he was holding out a hand, at once open and closed . . . he sent me a look that seemed to have been interrupted in its wandering . . . while I dug myself deeper and my fingers clutched in vain at the sand that continuously gave way, while I continued to labor away at climbing that interminable dune, more than half of which still remained before I would reach Mansour, then half of that distance followed by another half then half again and another half and so on into infinity . . . He had looked at me, then he had stood up on that dune, like a star stretching out, and had made from that straight line a curve, a circle, or maybe even an ellipse . . . Yes, an ellipse, leading from him to him passing through me. Or maybe not, he was already close to me when he straightened out, atop that dune I still saw as unattainable . . . he was already there, to lift me up while I continued to admire the star that he had become high above that dune, which at the time seemed to me to be the entire Earth. I seek the eyes of Mansour because they have the power to save us. *Gassouh! Gassouh!* I stood at Mansour's side, calm in the face of the unfolding of the sands and the rocks that sprawled the length of a red and ocher immensity below a sun giving off a soft glow that spread in long sweeps across the majestic cliffs of the Najd which also stretched out, rolled out in waves into dizzying escarpments that threaded their way across that vast expanse of sand, beyond which towered yet more majestic cliffs, like the two banks of the great river that flowed noisily centuries and centuries earlier and which had since become nothing more than a graceful and undulating succession of dunes, curved and dry and flowing toward the infinite that unfurled itself everywhere my eyes could turn . . .

3.

THE WIND WAS BLOWING hard that day. Stirring up the desert in every direction. I had parked the Camaro at roughly the same place as the previous time and had let Mansour return to that point, which he doubtless believed to be the same one as usual, on top of the same dune, so he could sit and stare, despite the wind, straight out in front of him. As for me, I remained in the car to smoke my hashish. I kept an eye on Mansour, up there on his dune, as if I needed to supervise him . . . less afraid that he might dash off into the void, where he would have just ended up huddled in a ball in the sand, and more that fate was bound to strike once again and cast over him an even darker cloud. Heaps of sand, carried about by the wind, hurled themselves against the windshield with a noise like a dry downpour. Out past Mansour, I could see the rocky plateau swept by violent gusts that whipped up clouds of dust, stone, earth, which shot into the air only to fall back down farther away, which is to say right here, too, on this long stretch of red dunes. And I imagined the gigantic masterpiece that was being assembled a stroke at a time before my very eyes, and before those of Mansour, which he held riveted on the sand, or so I assumed. Perhaps observing the millions, or the billions, rather, of grains, perhaps identifying them with the millions of neurons that made up his thinking matter, which is to say him, which is to say even more than his hands or his face or his eyes . . . even more than his entire body . . . Him, impalpable, the permanent and unquestionable feeling that he is not someone else . . . or something else. And it's most likely this, precisely this feeling, that tormented him in the face of that expanse of lifeless sand with which he was perhaps associating his mental state . . . while I sucked down the last puffs of my joint, continuing to observe him from the smoke-filled interior of the luxurious Camaro, observing him like that until the initial effects of the dope took hold, which led me to believe that Mansour must be self-identifying with a heap of sand . . . an agglomerate of sand sitting on a sand dune.

Within that deluxe leather interior, smoky and reeking of burnt wood, I took shelter from the wind's fury. I connected my iPhone to the Camaro's speakers to listen, in the very heart of the tumult, to Rasha Rizk's incredible voice. The majesty of the setting, the storm, and the combined effects of the dope and Rasha's songs carried me away toward sweet reveries which gave me an immediately physical pleasure. A roiling sensation moved its way through my head and a numbness soldered my entire body to the seat of the car. A consensual prisoner to all of these sensations, I let their caresses envelop the stone I had become . . . only my eyes kept a relative mobility so as to admire the expanse of dunes stretching off to one side and the cliffs to the other, to occasionally look in on the mineral agglomerate that Mansour had become, or at my legs, which I could no longer feel . . . the wind continued to hurl itself against the windows like pails of sand that my eyes attempted to follow . . . streaks of sand that formed into vortexes up above the dunes then descended toward the road on their way to slam against the car, exploding and dispersing into thousands of grains only to reassemble, by some miracle, into another vortex that went off down the other side of the road, toward the other expanse of dunes and then on to make its way up one of them and fly apart at its summit and disperse once again into thousands of grains that flitted about high above the entire expanse, as if blasting off, torn free of gravity once and for all and gathered up by even stronger winds and higher winds to soar above the entire region, well beyond Ar Ruwaidhah and perhaps even past Jeddah . . . only to fall to earth on another rocky plateau and be fixed there under the effects of the heat. As if soldered by the rays of an uncompromising sun. And me, more and more devastated, crushed, ground-down, and yet visibly at the heart of this creation painted one brushstroke at a time . . . the creation of the Earth. I observed this back-and-forth from one side of the road to the other and retraced the trajectory, imagining the destiny of one grain of sand . . . namely one originating on the plateau of the Najd, born of a minuscule cracking that the cold would have yanked without a cry from the ground and then bowled along by the gentle morning breeze and then whipped aloft by a storm from the east and then brutally dispatched across the long expanse of the dunes, this depot, the temporary matter of our world, to remain there for a few moments or a few centuries and then to be snatched away once again by the storms out of the east and sent back toward other rocky plateaus to remain there, eternally or not, pinned down by the heat, as if melted by the rays of an eternally uncompromising sun. In this way the future imposed itself. For the centuries to come, these renovations were already underway, and nothing would remain of the imposing plateau that so proudly rose up before Mansour, who simply stared back, or so I imagined at the time, without opening his eyes or even lowering them . . . No, there would be nothing left of Riyadh nor any trace of the Najd . . .

In this way the future revealed itself, in a sweet reverie in the interior of a luxurious red Camaro, with force and conviction. And then, my mind almost no longer having the strength to organize the thoughts that sprang forth and my eyes almost as paralyzed as the rest of my body, no longer having the strength to follow the curvatures traced by the wind, I let myself drift into contemplation of the natural beauty that the desert knew how to so generously offer. The gentleness of the sensations that beset body and mind, alongside the well-being I felt at the contact with Rasha's voice, these forced me toward this contemplation of beauty—the good in seeing the beautiful and the beauty in being good—an equivalence that crossed the centuries without ever being eroded, one employed by Ibn Sina and al-Farabi to articulate, develop, and disseminate a philosophy alongside a religion that was strong, intelligent, one of beauty and love . . . an equivalence perhaps borrowed less from Aristotle than from Plotinus, the anti-Arab Arab, and of course leading back to Plato and Socrates themselves and likely leading back to other enlightened men . . . much further back, possibly leading back to the first glimmers of thought . . . leading back to the first human who sat his bum down on a rock or a dune and, even for a moment, stopped hunting or running away, just a moment to contemplate a landscape and to feel something strange travel through him then overwhelm him, and not likely having words yet . . . perhaps also leading back to the first glimmers of language . . . and perhaps language itself sprang forth from this shock . . . perhaps the first word was poetic . . . whatever the case, this human likely not having enough words to express all of the beauty and all of the good to be shared with his species, his ilk, still took them by the hand and led them to that same rock or that same dune; magic, he had felt then or he had maybe thought or he had already said . . . whatever the case, he made them park their asses as he had, which is to say made them sit a moment and take the time to see the beauty and feel the good . . . like listening to a song. Whatever the case, I remained seated and full of words, contemplative before the distribution, the undulation, the *sinuation* of the dunes and the rocks that sprawled the length of a red and ocher immensity alongside a sun descending and diffusing its gentle rays and spreading them wide and finally setting in long sweeps across the majestic cliffs of the Najd which also stretched out, rolled out, reproduced in waves forming gigantic and dizzying ridges or escarpments that threaded and dashed their way across that vast expanse of sand beyond which towered yet more majestic cliffs from another plateau like two banks two shorelines of the great river that must have flowed noisily centuries and centuries earlier and which had since become nothing more than a graceful and undulating and silent succession of dunes, curved and dry and flowing toward the infinite that unfurled itself everywhere my eyes could turn . . .

Gassouh! Gassouh! A love song. But all must perish. The vast river like the vast thoughts of Ibn Sina. From Rasha's beautiful voice to the cries of Al Safat Square. All is manifestly perishable within the unfolding of time. The car door opened and then abruptly shut, startling me and letting in a drift of sand.

Mansour looked at me and noticed the state I was in. From within that pathetic state, I nonetheless thought I could see tearstains on his cheeks. But I didn't have the strength to question him, hardly enough to say to myself: My God, what life is this? He said nothing, content to lower the volume and drive off. I checked out a short while later, lulled by Rasha's voice, somewhere between Ksour al-Moqbel and the entry checkpoint of the Governorate of Riyadh.

The following day, after having washed my face and drunk a coffee and having assured myself that the topography of the earth most certainly didn't take shape the way I had dreamed it the evening before, I dashed off to see Kingdom's neurologist. The same nurses welcomed me with the same Good morning Sir! and the long corridor of the department still seemed just as dark. I explained to one of them that I wanted to see Dr. Maarafi again without my friend present so that we could discuss things without any embarrassment . . . The nurse assured me that Dr. Maarafi always spoke without embarrassment and that of course I had the right to come back and see him again for further explanations but that I would have to wait until the end of his consultations. And so I waited, a long time, sitting on a bench, watching the comings and goings of the patients and the nurses, thinking again about Abdelkader, Mansour's illustrious ancestor, and recalling an episode of his life that had struck me as strange and perhaps had some connection to the illness of my dear friend. It was said that Abdelkader, he too, had observed (or had perhaps been afflicted by) a long period of muteness upon his arrival in Damascus, that he had remained in seclusion in a corner of the Umayyad Mosque, hardly taking any nourishment and going for the most part without sleep, without reading and without chanting, his eyes fixed on the ground . . . for many days and nights. Was it of the same order as what Mansour was living through? Like something hereditary . . . Was it maybe just temporary? Like a nasty virus that would stir up disorder in Mansour's head and then leave again just like that, the way it had come . . . and I would find my friend back to the way he had always been, melancholic, to be sure, but full of life. No!, Dr. Maarafi curtly replied. No, there is nothing viral about it and whether it is hereditary hasn't the least bit of importance . . . Allow me to repeat myself, there is unfortunately no treatment . . . The best thing to do was still to give up on seeking out the origins of the affliction and assist Mansour, whether it was me or his parents, with the terrible ordeal he was going to go through. I nevertheless felt the need to suggest treatments in France or the United States, but Dr. Maarafi dismissed the idea by reminding me that in our day medicine was the same, here or elsewhere, and that in Arabia we had the most modern methods, state of the art medical techniques . . . and moreover, we were even, us Arabs, trailblazers when it came to modern medicine . . . and then he concluded by asking me, without awaiting my answer, if I had ever heard of Ibn Sina. Not wanting to get into all of that and not wanting to give up on my hopes of helping Mansour, I tried to find out if it wasn't impossible that there had been an error or if Mansour might develop another kind of intelligence . . . different . . . and thus undetectable to the battery of tests to which he had been subjected . . . because I felt that, in spite of everything, Mansour sensed things and understood situations . . . in a different way, sure, but he understood something . . . Like he was reading signs in the curvatures of the dunes and letters among the serpentine meanderings of the sand . . . like he heard something in the movement of the winds . . . like he saw a meaning in the reddening of the sun . . . Because he always returned to me, descending from atop his dune, his eyes always luminous and his gaze backlit by something . . . Maarafi looked at me a long while, took out his prescription pad, scrawled something across it, tore off the sheet and held it out to me as he stood up. Take this for a few weeks. It will do you a lot of good . . . and take care of your friend! he told me as he opened the door to his examination room and shook my hand. Goodbye Sir!

Gassouh! Gassouh! the men continue to shout as they accompany you with their eyes and mouths toward the center of the world from which you will disappear . . . in spite of yourself, in spite of all that you are and all that you have been and in spite of all the life that flows within you and in spite of all that springs forth from you as life as well . . . *Gassouh!* the crowd continues to shout in spite of all that I can remember about you, Mansour, and about the illness that the judge didn't want to recognize, didn't even want to consider in spite of the courageous testimony, it must be said, of Maarafi, whom I had pulled from a consultation and thrown into the Camaro so we could race to the courthouse in time to locate the small office of Judge Abou Daoud al-Qassimi and prevent him from sign-ing the indictment for heresy . . . In that small lightless office, Maarafi had tried his best to explain that medically speaking Mansour could no longer be properly considered a man, that he only had the appearance of one, the exterior . . . that he should be considered more as an animal . . . like a donkey, he had specified . . . and that His Excellency the Judge had not been appointed by God to judge donkeys, he had unfortunately added. The judge's small office had seemed to contract and grow even darker. A small eight-by-eleven pane let through something that wasn't quite light but a kind of grayish glow that leaked, that poured in like dirty water, into the scantiness of that hole in which there was a shelf containing a dozen books and a prayer mat, in which there was also a table, three chairs, and an unlit floor lamp. I had the sensation that we were at the bottom of a well while Maarafi continued to develop his argument before the impassible and ageless face of the judge, who intermittently readjusted the ample headscarf, white and immaculate, with which he covered his head . . . while Maarafi, in turn, readjusted his argumentation in accordance with the look given him by the judge so as to convince him. To save what remained of Mansour, of the man . . . because in spite of everything there was something left, at least a story, at least a name, at least a soul . . . a breath. Or were we at the bottom of a tomb when Judge Qassimi had straightened up, adjusted once more the large folds of his white *shemagh*, then had begun to speak . . . He to whom God has not granted light, what light shall he have? he seemed to ask by citing the Qur'an and lowering his eyes toward his hands, which he had moved forward to rest on the table. Then he went back over Maarafi's explanation point by point, explaining that indeed he had not been appointed by God to judge donkeys. That the will of God, manifested through destiny, had in some way brought about the meeting of our trajectories for us to arrive where we were . . . Ambroise Paré once said, *You treat him and God heals him,* to respond to Maarafi, and as you might easily guess, I do not judge bodies but minds and souls. You have just explained clearly to me that his body ails from an incurable illness and without a doubt his mind and his soul will be involuntarily eaten away by it, and so it falls upon me, unavoidably, to save these . . . Then he brought his hands back toward him, joined them together on his chest, and began to recite a verse from the Qur'an . . . *Light upon light! God guides to His light whom He wills. Allah is the Light of the heavens and the earth. The example of His light is like a niche within which is a lamp* . . . Then he interrupted himself, tried to pick up his previous phrase again but the word Light seemed to leave him in an uncomfortable position, unexpected and uncontrollable . . . Overtaken by emotion . . . a lump in his throat . . . overwhelmed by emotion . . . no longer able to speak aloud . . . then he took a deep breath, and finally managing to collect himself . . . *The lamp is within glass, the glass as if it were a shining star . . . kindled from a blessed tree. An olive neither of the East nor of the West, whose oil would almost glow forth though no fire touched it* . . . Then once again overtaken by emotion, and finally overwhelmed . . . he finally succumbed, crying, sobbing, breaking off and then picking up again at the last phrase and then sobbing all over again, uncontrollably . . . without being able to complete his verse . . . he then hastily rose to his feet and left the office. Fleeing. Was it the meaning of the verse that was bringing tears to his eyes or was it the sound of the words or was it the gravity of his decision? We had no idea . . . In silence, and completely puzzled, Maarafi and I awaited his return so as to know what the future held for Mansour . . . but he never came back. After never-ending minutes in the dark of that small office, an employee noticed us as he made his rounds through the halls of the courthouse. Can't stay here, he told us, the judge has gone home. I dropped Maarafi off without a word in front of Kingdom Hospital and felt, for the first time, the need to go out to the dunes. Facing a reddening sun, the Camaro floated along Mekkah Road to leave Riyadh and the Najd plateau, to pass its dizzying escarpments and to seek out a meaning to ascribe to those unexpected sobs. But how is one to know? How is one to know anything at all?

In the distance, beyond the dunes, the cliffs of the Najd emerged from the fog of sand that had sheltered them for a time, appearing to us like the ruins of an ancient Greek or Roman metropolis . . . the cuts that the centuries and the climate's severity had made to those rocky pediments, beyond the dunes atop of which crawled sinuous shadows, they inevitably led us to see ancient Palmyra . . . the ruins of Palmyra . . . the ruins of the ruins of Palmyra. And perhaps Mansour, from his eyes, saw neither Palmyra nor its ruins nor the ruins of any Greek metropolis, but simply the first circle of a series of circles that would bring about his ascension . . . on the horizon, the cliffs of the Najd squeezed one against the next in the arc of a circle, the remains of a circle to which Mansour's stationary position, which is to say the exact point that he spent so long finding atop his dune, was the exact center . . . like what Abdelkader had set out to do when he moved his entire *smala* across an earth full of fire and blood, spending long minutes, even long hours, looking for the point, the center, within a silence that he had managed to impose on all of them. Then the entire *smala* came to life again around that gravitational center where he had commanded his tent be raised and around which a first circle of tribes circulated then a second circle of tribes and so on . . . and not only for reasons of military strategy, of protocol or of Arab aesthetics, but also to adhere as closely as possible to that science of enlightenment inherited from his father, from his grandfather, and so on all the way to the greatest of masters, son of Plato and oneiric confidant of Aristotle, and next to whom he wished to rest for eternity, Muhyi al-Din ibn ʿArabi. Eternity, if not for the decision to repatriate Abdelkader's ashes so as to construct myths and erect statues . . . eternity, if not for the decision of the new president of that new state in that new world that was

taking shape and of which we already understood so little . . .
So perhaps Abdelkader held fast to that science of forms and
numbers like it was a sort of mooring, a foundation, a religion
within the religion, that science of numbers and forms wherein
the first circle of tribes was made up of four tents and the second of seven then the next of fourteen . . . and so on it went
with only him knowing the arithmetical progression, which he
still remembered when he finally came near the ashes of Ibn
ʿArabi, sitting in a simple corner of the Umayyad Mosque and
maybe, at that very moment, struck dumb and wiped clean by
the blows of fate or, on the contrary, at peace and filled with
something else . . .

. . . from a corner, then, necessarily constituting the center of
everything, from that angle in the Umayyad Mosque, Abdelkader
relinquished himself to an arithmetical and geometrical understanding of things while during that same era Henri Poincaré
was starting out at the Polytechnique to learn all truth, in its
totality, and to bring a close to that line of exceptional beings
and in a way to be the final seal of the great universal scholars,
to end up becoming the last to know all of mathematics in their
totality and to be at the origin of the greatest theories of the
modern era before universal understanding itself exploded into
an indescribable chaos like billions of billions of grains of sand
hurled in the direction and in the face of billions of pairs of eyes
that were powerless when it came to understanding anything
that is or that was in this word become definitively incomprehensible . . .

The wind having subsided, all that remained was a fog of
dust that dissipated behind him as he walked back toward me
to announce his big news. Leaving the summit of his dune like

an ascetic returning from a harrowing retreat . . . returning
spent, his gaze wiped blank . . . returning from the winds and
the sands . . . out of breath and eyes reddened . . . but I didn't
have the strength to question him, in spite of the tearstains, nor
to tell myself, My God, what life is this? Wordlessly, he was
content to lower the volume and bring the engine to life, to fly
back down that path, and as we ate up the miles, he found the
breath that his voice had been lacking to tell me that a woman
would come to cure him. A woman with big eyes lined with
kohl, with hair curly like the waves of a troubled sea and with
a direct gaze, solid and fixed like an anchorage . . . or like an
archangel, was that what he said? Big eyes that would open his
own. I checked out a short while later, lulled by Rasha's voice,
somewhere between Ksour al-Moqbel and the entry checkpoint of the Governorate of Riyadh.

Gassouh! Gassouh! Like unending thunder in the dust-filled
sky over Al Safat Square where hideous faces, deformed by
hatred, are now turning toward Judge Abou Daoud al-Qassimi,
who advances without a sob in your wake, Mansour, to assume
responsibility for his judgment right up until the end and to be
the privileged witness of your obliteration from the surface of
this land on which we washed up without really wanting to.
This land that constantly grows from the motes of dust that fall
without end by the billion, by the billions of billions . . . and
you know, Mansour, I went there too . . . Your beautiful red
Camaro deposited me at the foot of your dune, after having
dropped Maarafi in front of the Kingdom and having crossed all
of Riyadh under a sky that seemed black to me, and I placed my
footsteps in yours and I climbed back up that hill of sand and
I searched for that point from which it seemed to me that you
saw the truth stripped bare . . . but did I truly find it, that point?

Because all around me, there was nothing but desert. Emptiness as far as the eye could see. And I told myself that perhaps this was what you had come looking for, not the infinite beauty of that empty infinite, but the passage through the immediate beauty of the desert to reach its emptiness and take refuge within it. Mansour, you were falling from atop that dune into an unfathomable void without my even being able to notice it happening. And I remained like that a long while, Mansour, standing there in the winds, trying to understand what had happened to you and how I could have done that to you and how you could have said that and what al-Qassimi's sobs meant . . . but how is one to understand anything when the dryness of the wind is burning one's skin? How is one to know within the smoky leather interior of a Camaro that is sailing down the desert's paths? How is one to know, lost somewhere between Rasha's voice and the lights of Riyadh? . . . Much like Abdelkader, alone in a corner of the Umayyad Mosque, burnoose fallen back on his head and gaze lost on the surface of the cold tiles, without speaking without drinking without eating and even without moving . . . perhaps you dwelled there, Mansour, atop your dune, your gaze lost in the desert's immensity, in the hope of bringing an end to the agonizing concerns of knowledge and understanding. Abdelkader's eye stuck on the geometrical forms of the tiling, the mosaics or the ornamentation of that great mosque which had in some ways been the outward expression of Islam's grandeur, stuck amid the squares and starry polygons, stuck amid the complexity of the symmetry and of the rotations of the tessellations, stuck and turning endlessly around the circumferences of the circles, without end and without exit, lost the way one gets lost in the desert and taking shelter for one's mind, so to speak, within that higher and divine intelligence so as to maybe appease his soul because he could not comprehend why the tribes had abandoned him nor why the Duke of Aumale had betrayed his word nor why Napoléon III had held him prisoner for so long, no more than he would understand, later on, that same Napoléon's intense friendship and the eagerness of France to decorate him, to photograph him, to exhibit him, and he also wouldn't have understood, even if he had lived as long as Abraham or Moses, the plundering of the country to which he had in a manner of speaking given birth, nor its destruction and ruin by the dark hordes who pillaged and killed in the name of Islam.

4.

AND THEN CAME THE EVENING of the big reception at the French
embassy and the bundle of hopes that came with it. As I was
in the Economic Services department's good books, I had the
privilege of honoring the French Ambassador with my presence on December 30, 2013, at the residence of His Excellency,
for a reception given in honor of the visit of the President of
the French Republic, François Hollande, and his entire retinue
of ministers. I of course took Mansour with me, telling myself
that he would enjoy seeing some people and, above all, having
some drinks. And so we arranged to meet at 7 p.m. in the
Diplomatic Quarter, and we started out with a long wait in the
lineup of invited guests that stretched around the walls of the
residence. This included French expats and all those whom, like
us, had some routine connection to France. A large majority
were Lebanese but also a few Saudis and a handful of North
Africans whom we ran into regularly at the monthly social
organized by the embassy to give everyone a breather from the

prying eyes of the Kingdom's authorities. Once we were inside the residence, we stood in another line to shake the hand of Monsieur, the Ambassador, then that of Madame and then we made a break for the already packed buffet. We still managed to take two glasses of wine each and escape the throng by heading for a giant tent put up for the occasion, where the President was to give his speech. At that point we had the great fortune of running into a certain dickhead from Cultural Services I knew, overexcited, way too pumped up, and he cried out: Hussein! You old ballsack! Ahh, all this exceedingly French tenderness! Made up of gentle vulgarities to mark attachment (we're all quite attached to our balls) and proximity (we're never very far away from our balls) . . . At any rate, he made sure to have us seated inside the tent, in the first row, among the big-name guests . . . but without the two glasses of wine that were helping us to weather the storm, to unwind a bit, and which we had to grudgingly abandon. Placed between the head of Airbus and the head of Alstom, we remained standing, just opposite the stage and the microphone, as we waited for the arrival of the man who rumor had it was already in the residence gardens. And this turned out to be true, a few minutes later, when Hollande finally appeared under the big top to applause, with the group of ministers that had accompanied him following in his wake . . . Fabius, Montebourg, Le Drian, and the immortal Jack Lang . . . and perhaps others as well but whose names or faces I didn't recognize. Behind me, I heard amused voices that were surprised not to see Prime Minister Ayrault . . . I heard *Ayro! Ayro!* with a Lebanese accent and instantly understood their little joke. *Ayro* meaning "dick" in our region, some regretted the absence of this man who would have seemed like he was a part of them, so easy to feel attached to, such a big softy . . .

His face sweaty but smiling, Hollande greeted the audience and began his speech: *Ladies and gentlemen, this is the second time that I have come to Saudi Arabia since being elected. The first was in November 2012, when I met with King Abdullah, in Jeddah. Together, we agreed to an official visit over the course of 2013 and as such, I am here, with you, at this beautiful residence, during these the final days of the year. Our bilateral relations are excellent. These are tied to our history first of all, because for decades France and Saudi Arabia have worked together toward a certain number of principles on the international stage . . .* After having expressed his wish, most cherished, he had said, to meet with the French community and thank it for its engagement and determination when it came to the execution and promotion of French *savoir-faire* and excellence along the different lines of cooperation that he had felt it important to enumerate, which of course were exclusively economic, financial, and military, which the heads of industry had not hesitated to greet with interest and satisfaction, François Hollande had thanked us as well, we, the Lebanese, Syrians, and Middle Easterners in whose hearts France dwelled and who were present this evening in such a beautiful residence, always open to its friends . . . he turned toward Fabius, who stood motionless, as straight as the letter I and as rigid as a statue, his hands behind his back and his eyes fixed on the ground and thus not noticing the attention focused his way, yet revealing at that precise moment a fixed grin as if he could feel that the president was looking at him . . . Astonishing! Astonishing, these great men with their intellects as rational as they were sensitive . . . In any case, at that point I had felt certain that we were about to get to the heart of the speech. *But if I come to Saudi Arabia, it is not solely—and this is already very important—to promote the exceptionality of France, it is also because we have a political relationship of the highest order. In the company of the king, this afternoon, we followed to their conclusion all of the discussions on regional subjects that we felt could be of use. I appreciate the wisdom of King Abdullah, it is precious in such moments, because he demonstrates that he is willing to do what it takes to find solutions. Security is the main question. How to allow us to achieve even greater security in the region. It isn't a question of going on the offensive, it is first and foremost about security . . . Has Bashar al-Assad not been playing a game, one in which he makes use of extremists to justify the campaign of repression that he has so unfortunately carried out upon his own people even in recent days, with the terrible bombings that have taken place in Aleppo?* A question directed to himself and which had the effect of snapping Fabius out of his grinning torpor. At this, he had immediately turned toward the president, uncrossing his hands from his back so as to subtly bring an index finger to rest on his cheek . . . Quite astonishing, this language used by great men who also communicate with signs and glances. I then attentively watched Fabius's eyes and was struck by their strange color . . . not blue, not gray but maybe both at the same time, they truly appeared metallic . . . he held that cold and metallic gaze while the president answered his own question: *My answer is yes, the objective alliance between these forces is a game, one intended to render the country incapable of finding a solution. France and Saudi Arabia, in regard to Syria, much as in regard to other questions of international affairs, but notably when it comes to Syria, share exactly the same position, and that is the desire to search for a political solution, to support the moderate opposition and encourage a transition. It is on that basis that for the past few months we have been acting together. I am aware of the important role played by Saudi Arabia, particularly when it comes to backing the national Syrian coalition. And this role has been extremely invaluable. I am aware of what Saudi Arabia has done in the fight against extremism, which I have stated can, at the end of the day, be considered an accomplice to Bashar al-Assad's regime. At the Geneva Conference, we have to work together toward the result that I have described. This must not be the prolongation of Bashar al-Assad. You know what the position of France was the moment chemical weapons were used. Because chemical weapons have been employed in Syria, there is no longer any debate about this, they have been employed. Such a reprehensible act definitively condemns this regime in the eyes of the world, and France is ready, adhering to its duty to protect civilian life, to punish those who made the odious decision to gas innocent people.* At this, Fabius reassumed his initial stance. Crossed his hands behind his back, kept his eyes half-closed and fixed on the ground, and sporadically grinned his fixed grin, the signification of which only he seemed to know. Almost a kind of meditation, I thought, while President Hollande continued to speak about my country. I had, of course, a few reservations when it came to his analysis of the situation, but I didn't get too worked up about it because, all things considered, his speech wasn't meant to initiate a debate but was instead a sort of debriefing of what had already been decided, between Saudi Arabia and France, concerning the fate of my country. *It is the pressure we have exerted, that of France, that of Saudi Arabia, that has brought about the beginning of the destruction of these chemical weapons. But today, there are bombings taking place over Aleppo, which affects the civilian population, and further massacres are being perpetrated. And so we have both adopted exactly the same position and we want to bring this terrible situation to a conclusion. Not only for Syria, but for the entire region, taking into account what we know about refugees, in Lebanon—of which we have spoken—with the risk of a deterioration of the situation in that friendly country. And then, refugees who may also leave the region, and we all know the difficulties this can engender, including for Europe, and so we are in precisely the same position.* At this, the audience demonstrated, via a sort of rippling swell, its approval and its satisfaction.

I took advantage of this brief unruliness to check how things were going with my friend . . . I leaned forward slightly and discreetly turned my head so that I could see Mansour and what I saw almost made me burst out laughing. I held myself back, biting my tongue, eyes plunging to the ground, but despite this I could still picture the clownish smile that Mansour was deliberately aiming at the French leader. A grotesque smile that Hollande had most certainly not failed to notice but which didn't seem to bother him . . . And yet it was such a grotesque smile, bordering on a grimace. Imperturbable, Hollande went on: *As to the relations between Saudi Arabia and Lebanon, it is the sovereignty of these two nations that is being challenged. I am not here to discuss that with you today. What I do know is that France, for a long time now, but even more so in recent times, has equipped the Lebanese army and will not turn a deaf ear to any requests addressed to it. Why? Because as I have said, Lebanon must remain stable, its integrity must be respected. Its security must be assured, for all Lebanese citizens, for all of the components that make up Lebanese life, for Lebanon as a whole. I therefore maintain my relationship with President Suleiman, who I've been in contact with recently, and if there are requests made of us, we will meet them.* I heard, right then, coming from the rear of the tent, candid expressions of relief and satisfaction immediately followed by unexpected applause. Fabius reopened his metallic eyes and found a grin appropriate to the circumstances. To silence the applause, Hollande gave a great smile, opened wide his hands and stretched them out before him, and took up his speech again, by way of conclusion, to talk about employment in France and the need to increase trade with Arabia. Fabius took his leave at this point, without waiting for the end of the speech, to a dirty look from Montebourg and Le Drian's eternally smiling gaze . . . I wanted to follow him and head straight for the buffet but I was in the front row and did not have Fabius's official standing. I bided my time, which turned out to be a long while since I was no longer listening to the president but distractedly looking at the head of his personal security detail. A woman with constantly moving eyes, nervous, and with a body that one would imagine to be equally nervous, taut and well-muscled . . . so nothing to hope for there. Daydreaming, I looked over the various members of the government, I examined their bearings, turning my attention back to the speech, at least intermittently, when there was laughter from the audience in response to the jokes and quips which were clearly President Hollande's strong suit, and which he was able to skillfully pepper in amid all the gravitas. A new round of applause signaled the end of the speech and as we made a beeline to retrieve our glasses of wine and empty them on our way to acquire some more . . . at that exact moment, that same dickhead grabbed me by the arm, Woah woah woah there, ballsack!, insisting that we have our photo taken with the president. Held by the arm and pushed, along with Mansour, up to the foot of the stage from which the president stepped down to position himself between Mansour and me while the little dickhead took the photo . . . the temptation was too strong and we couldn't prevent ourselves, neither one of us, from reproducing that same idiotic smile, which the dickhead showed us immediately afterward, asking us, still in the presence of the president, if we were happy with the photo . . . I hurried to say Perfect! at the same time that Hollande, who had clearly noticed our mockery, asked Mansour if he wasn't feeling well: Is it some discomfiture that makes you smile that way? While preventing my friend from answering by pulling him by the arm, I welcomed the president to Saudi Arabia, and half-dragged, half-pushed Mansour into the middle of the crowd of people waiting their turn for a selfie destined to serve as a screenshot for a computer or a cell phone or both . . . we did, quite fortunately, lose the dickhead in the middle of that same crowd and soon we arrived at a buffet that was relatively unpopulated. Glasses of wine finally in hand, we allowed drunkenness to pleasantly overtake us as we contemplated the throng that was forming around the head of state, who was painstakingly advancing, his smile painted on all the while, and I told Mansour that the photo ops were likely going to take him the rest of the night, by the look of the hundred people who were waiting. I asked him, as we stood in the crowd, what had come over him to make him smile so idiotically . . . a smile so idiotic that it had become infectious. Mansour did little to alleviate my suspicion that he had been deliberately mocking when he assured me he only meant to reproduce a smile that the president himself had worn on some other occasion and which he had seen on the internet, thinking he could return it to him like one would return a salute . . . Little by little, the guests who had succeeded in having their photo taken came to join us around the buffet table to satisfy their hunger but above all their thirst, standing in front of the white tablecloths that presented us with nothing better than Red Label or Clan Campbell, Martini Rosso or Bianco, gin or vodka, lower-tier Bordeaux and room-temperature beer . . . but that was always the way of it and we were all very grateful.

As I kept an eye on Mansour who was asking the waiter to refill our two glasses, which we would then drink rather quickly, my gaze crossed that of a woman whom I found to be extremely beautiful. Nadine, I would later find out she was called, was rather simply dressed for such a reception . . . jeans, blouse, and linen jacket . . . shoulder-length hair cut in a bob, curled and skillfully mussed up . . . no jewelry and no makeup, and yet she shone, to my eyes. As I approached her, I noticed a touch of kohl around her eyes and a light red to her lips but also, not without a twinge in my heart, a husband at her side. A pleasant-looking husband, fortunately. *Venez vous joindre*! he threw at us in poor beginner's French when he caught sight of us, Mansour and me, looking lost and maybe a bit restless . . . Pulling myself together, I grabbed my friend and soon the four of us were deep into the introductions and then in full conversation . . . In fact, it was Stan who took charge of the conversation; chatting garrulously and draining his drinks rather quickly, he directed our volleys like a true coach, which it turned out he was . . . Nadine, quiet, curiously stared at Mansour, who still appeared lost, looking successively at his glass his feet the people and the walls of the residence . . . and me, tightrope walker that I am, I admired Nadine's face and, as best I could, sometimes in English sometimes in French, pulled the wool over the eyes of Stan the Australian ex-tennis champion, a Francophile, he told us, who had since become an athletics trainer for wealthy Saudis who wanted to stay in shape. I also tried to attract Nadine's attention by showing myself to be *tellement amusant* and by trying to be *si intelligent* but nothing managed to divert her gaze from Mansour, who continued peacefully, off in his own little world, to put back drink after drink . . . I even managed to buttonhole the Eternal Jack as he walked past us at one point and I even managed to make him laugh and to suck him into a discussion about mineralogy in the oceanic plates of the Gulf, but nothing, absolutely nothing, was able to divert Nadine's attention away from poor—and likely already drunk—Mansour. I let Jack go free to resume, like a satellite in zero gravity, his trajectory around other clusters of people and I surrendered, not without regret, before the black hole that my friend had become and that held prisoner all of Nadine's light.

Gassouh! Gassouh! What a trajectory, Mansour! What a trajectory! I only now understand that what brought you close to Nadine, nothing could have pulled you back away . . . what brought you close to her brought you closer to yourself than you could have ever been on your own. They are gravitational forces so powerful that nothing and nobody could have changed the trajectory. And what a trajectory! From the halls of the French residence to this square, so noisy and so hostile . . . My God the hostility! Nothing and nobody, oh God, would have been able to curve the straight line that you travel . . . and you will bend forward beneath the blade the same way that a rock falls to earth . . . My God, what a trajectory! And I ask your forgiveness, Mansour, for having momentarily wished for your head when Nadine was avoiding my gaze to attract your eyes . . . I beg your forgiveness, Mansour!

Nadine Nasr-Vaughan asked Mansour, in Arabic, if he was also Lebanese. Sort of . . . he replied, without ever really climbing out of his lost state or his drunkenness. She seemed contented enough with his reply seeing as she asked for no further clarification. Did she simply want to hear his voice? Who is to say? I went off to get refills for everyone. When I returned, I noticed that a strange muteness had fallen over the three of them . . . Mansour was looking at Stan who was looking at Nadine who was looking at Mansour . . . I distributed the drinks and Stan asked us what we did for a living. I was explaining that we worked for a property development firm, me as an engineer, and Mansour as an architect, when my friend interrupted me to specify that he had lost his job and was looking for a new one . . . that his training having been more in landscape design he hoped to undertake a career as a gardener. Which triggered great hilarity from Stan but also his generosity, because he instantly proposed that Mansour begin his beautiful and glorious new career in their garden . . . to which my friend replied favorably, but volunteered at the same time one reservation, seeing as he was looking for a job that came with accommodation and meals, with *gîte et couvert*, he had said at first in French, to Stan's incomprehension . . . to which Nadine also replied favorably, especially seeing that they had, at their villa, a little outbuilding that would do the trick perfectly after a few adjustments . . . to which Mansour replied, *Oui, d'accord* . . . after which Stan got out his cell phone to type in Mansour's number, held out his hand and said, *Merde!* It's a deal, you asshole! out of some sort of tenderness . . . and of course with proximity and attachment. As for me, I needed nothing more than my eyes to observe the gravitational forces that bind stars together, and the inexorable trajectories that they follow.

From that point on, the series of events occurred following a rather hazy and rather incoherent progression. The liquor was seriously interfering with our vision and our hearing and pushed us toward happenings that we would surely feel embarrassed about the following day. While the other three went back to their enigmatic muteness, I attempted to follow Jack's trajectory with my eyes, trying to catch a glimpse of his cards as he went about French diplomacy . . . Nevertheless, I understood that *Monsieur* Jack Lang, so comfortable and so similar to the rest of the executives in his gestures and his speech, was not only along on the trip to represent the *Institut du Monde Arabe*. Perhaps he was there to step in for Fabius, who was visibly tired and had promptly withdrawn from this little shindig? Who is to say? Simple to spot thanks to his hair, as black and distinctive as it was, my friend Jack was easy to follow in his peregrinations, shifting seamlessly and without interruption from discussions with the heads of industry to accolades with Le Drian to chuckles with Montebourg and to peals of laughter in the company of the representatives of the realm, which is to say the princes and the deputy princes and the crown princes and the deputy crown princes and the deputy crown deputy princes . . . and so on until there was no longer a trace of him, the alcohol seriously impairing my sight and my sense of direction. Immobile, I lost myself trying to follow Jack's amazing hair and Nadine's unbelievable eyes at the same time . . . And at that very moment, the alcohol overwhelmed Mansour's stomach most of all, which emptied itself noisily all over Stan's suit. A woman screamed in revulsion at the sight of the yellowish geyser spurting in fits and starts from my friend's mouth, and Stan, paradoxically, belted out his admiration regarding his new employee. *Merde!* I love this asshole! As best we could, Stan and I hurried to haul Mansour out into the residence's gardens where he continued, a heave at a time, to empty his stomach all over the beds of flowers that they had miraculously brought to life at this latitude, where we suffocated all year long . . . The embassy guards—sporty young men with short-cropped hair, in suits and typically wearing smiles in all circumstances—charged at us, not smiling at all, asking us if we please wouldn't mind clearing the hell off . . . As I was asking myself if the formula "to not mind clearing the hell off" might qualify as an oxymoron,

François Hollande, who had only then finished his round of selfies and who had witnessed "the incident," approached us to ask if everything was all right and if he could be of any sort of help . . . which drew over, of course, half the guests, who all squeezed in to admire Mansour on his knees, Stan holding him by the shoulders, Nadine wiping off his face, the little dickhead hiding his own face in his hands, and me, negotiating with the guards in hopes of a respectable exit for the group of us . . . and thus half the guests all had the opportunity to admire the large and grotesque smile, some might say idiotic, that François Hollande directed our way as we took our leave, the four of us, flanked quite closely by the best of the guards.

Outside, things were still just as chaotic . . . Nadine's stare boring a hole into me when I insisted I would accompany Mansour home and then Nadine's voice expressing her desire for Stan to accompany us both and Mansour crying out his refusal and Nadine's hands encircling Mansour's taut face as he kept refusing to allow the humiliation go that far and Stan's firm hand above Mansour's cringing face and then the hugs between Stan and Mansour and me that went on right up until a vehicle full of Saudi soldiers came to a stop beside us. The driver lowered his window and asked if everything was all right and then the car drove off after they had heard Stan assure them in English, Okay! Okay! Everything's all right! And then at that, Nadine's stare as it turned away and her face as it disappeared into Stan's dimly lit 4x4 and the sound of the doors as they slammed and then the fading sound of the engine . . . and then Mansour at the wheel of his beautiful red Camaro and then me in my car, behind, trailing the taillights of that beautiful red Camaro as it flew toward its destiny along the highways of Riyadh. That's how the night ended, or, at least, the conscious recollection we had of that soiree . . . because we just drove, one behind the other, completely wasted and without the least bit of self-awareness, as if following some sort of trajectory. For that matter, we had no idea, when we awoke in our own beds, how we were still alive. We had purely and simply been towed along by powerful gravitational forces. That evening had had its bundle of hopes in the person of François Hollande, who promised to save our country either directly or via Lebanon, and in the person of Stan, who had promised to hire Mansour and who, visibly, had enough physical strength to take him in hand . . . and then, there had been the face and the eyes and the voice of Nadine, which I hoped to see turn in my direction one day. But upon waking, after having thanked the guardian angels who had transported me to my bed, I was no longer all that sure about anything at all.

Gassouh! Gassouh! It's toward these cries that the gravitational forces pulled you, Mansour . . . and nothing and nobody could have changed the destination or diminished the strength of that attraction. Will François appear among all these hate-filled faces? Will he laugh his head off after a clever joke? A cutting jibe? Or will he at long last find the strong bearing of the president of France and the diction to go with it? Or maybe François le Français, defender of human rights, will smile at you again, one last time, to show you his compassion, his regret, and his firm condemnation? I don't think so, Mansour. We understood nothing of the world or its fall from grace. We thought we could see the intentions of the powerful for what they were, but neither one of us had the intelligence or the intuition to have a hope of understanding anything at all about anything at all.

5.

Very quickly, Mansour found himself in Stan and Nadine's employ. Having abandoned job and apartment, he from that point lived in a small outbuilding near their large villa, among the scorched plants and flowers of the garden. The sun, the dryness, the heat and the absence of upkeep had ended up leaving everything charred and giving that elegant courtyard the look of a field of despair. Mansour had even said that it reminded him of the strange prairie from his dream and that all that was missing for him to feel fully back there again was the ass . . . to which I replied, inevitably and inwardly, that he would suffice as a stand-in for the ass. Very quickly, Mansour found himself in Stan and Nadine's employ . . . and, to go into specifics, everything was arranged over a span of three days, made to seem like one single long day by my excessive drug use. We were returning from a trip out into the desert where Mansour, as was his custom, had gone off in isolation to enter into communion with I have no idea what, while I, as was my custom, had remained in isolation in the Camaro and within the cloud of hashish smoke to enter into communion with myself, or so I had pretentiously thought. And so, heading back in and then ringing the bell at the large villa, we saw Stan open the door for us and demonstrate his joy by shouting to Nadine, somewhere within the house, that those two assholes had arrived . . . Hunched over, I followed Mansour who followed Stan, looking at him as if he didn't truly exist . . . as if Stan possessed no human qualities, as if he were no more than mobile and sonorous matter that led us toward the living room and its deep armchairs, where we settled in to await the drinks he had promised us. I felt more and more hunched over, as if bowing under my own weight. I gradually sank into the large leather armchair and tried desperately to cling to reality by watching, through the room's bay window, the comings and goings of Stan and Nadine's chauffeur, as he circled a brown 4x4 parked in the courtyard. Stan appeared and disappeared with regularity without my knowing the exact reason, and Mansour was constantly staring at me, also without my knowing the reason. I avoided his stare by continuing to observe the comings and goings of the driver and the furnishings of the living room, which I considered to be pretty tasteless and which conflicted with what I'd picked up on about Nadine as far as style and refinement went. Stan finally returned with the desperately awaited drinks and promptly closed the curtains of the bay window. Those assholes would send you to the gallows for the five hundred riyals! he confided as he invited us to share both his caution and a sampling of the *vin maison* that he made himself in the basement, access to which was utterly forbidden to the Pakistani, Ikram, who served as Nadine's driver. It was true that Ikram kept a constant eye on us as he cleaned the

4x4, like he expected to see something interesting or like he suspected something serious was afoot . . . or quite simply out of curiosity, I had told myself. Stan held out to us the fruit of his labors, cloudy and reeking of alcohol, and asked us where we were arriving from. Incapable of replying in any audible way, I left it to Mansour to take care of things. From the desert, he said concisely. And why's that? pursued Stan, but Mansour didn't answer, or not really, muttering something like, No reason, which clearly had no effect when it came to dissuading Stan, who, in search of a topic of conversation, had hit on a good one. You watch yourselves! There's something bewitching out there . . . A friend of his, an expat like him and like the whole lot of us, actually, used to go out there quite frequently and once he left Saudi Arabia and returned to England, he missed the desert so much that he tried a thousand different ways, any way you can imagine, to get a visa so he could return and see the dunes of the Najd . . . but obviously, no visa and he hadn't been able to come back. Sad and desperate, he only found comfort in spending entire evenings watching all kinds of Westerns on TV, paying close attention to the noisy cavalcades as they rode from the cliffs of the Grand Canyon to the wide sands of New Mexico, in the hope of finding a bit of that lost magic once again . . . his wife grew tired of him and his depression cost him his job. It didn't take long for him to find himself all alone, watching shitty Westerns from morning till night in the company of a goldfish with which he said he could communicate through signs . . . despite my repeat attempts to find out more about these mysterious signs, I lost the thread of the conversation and returned to mechanically following the comings and goings of the driver, on the other side of the bay window, up until the moment that Nadine made her entrance into the living room. Her entrance and her exit, actually, because she hardly greeted us and hurriedly pulled Mansour away by the arm to introduce him to Ikram and to arrange, between the three of them, how and when they would collect all of his things so as to have him moved in as quickly as possible. Vivacious and beautiful enough to die for, Nadine clarified that she would go out immediately to purchase everything she thought Mansour would need so that he would feel comfortable, so that he felt at home, or even better than he had been in his own place . . . Nadine, like a slap that instantly tore me from my torpor and from the armchair into which I had sunk only to find myself watching them from behind the curtain of the bay window, spying on them, while Stan just stood there firmly planted in the middle of the living room, his drink in his hand, offering me a smile that I wasn't quite able to interpret. Was he still under the effects of that slap and was he still smiling at me or had he gone back to telling me the story about his friend while I turned back to the curtains and observed them—they say that spirits haunt those dunes—while Nadine continued to hold Mansour by the arm—that it's somehow the place where all of the spirits on earth congregate—while her lips moved as Ikram looked stormily on with a look that I found strange and intolerant, to say the least, sizing things up in an underhanded way, compared to that of Nadine, which to me appeared straight and resolute and open and irresistibly beautiful as it focused on Mansour's gleaming eyes, who then turned to Ikram and held out his hand, which the other man then listlessly took in his own to shake it just as listlessly as he looked away from Nadine's unbelievable face even as I asked myself how it was possible to turn away from that face for a single instant and since Stan was still behind me—spirits that sometimes end up inhabiting certain men—waiting for I don't know what to become clear about the whole scene that I continued to observe in spite of everything . . . in spite of the indecency, in spite of the impropriety, in spite of the fear and in spite of the tearing, the lightning bolt that shot through me when Nadine took her leave of Ikram and again clung to Mansour as she accompanied him like he was an invalid back inside and to the living room where Stan and I, turned to stone, hadn't moved a muscle—spirits that ended up inhabiting some of us to never leave again. Nadine gently pushed Mansour toward the center of the room and went off to do her shopping. Mansour advanced toward us as if he was still driven by the slight momentum she had imparted to him before she left, leaving him to us as if a rolling ball.

Gassouh! Gassouh! And you stop moving forward, you raise your head and you open your eyes. But what do you see, Mansour? From your vantage point, Mansour, gaze fixed straight ahead of you but also elsewhere . . . can you see them shouting or do you see something else? Is there even something else to see, other than all this hatred and all this morbid curiosity that solders the crowd together, cramming us one against the next? And is it even possible to see something else? Is it possible to see something other than the center of this esplanade? You look and you smile, Mansour! Do you see Nadine's face or do you see that of someone else? What face do you see, Mansour? From atop that dune pummeled by the wind, you also saw something else . . . perhaps the billions of grains of sand, whipped up violently, formed something that only you could perceive . . . Some philosophers say that we need something greater than us to be able to go on living . . . Was that what you were searching for from the top of that dune, which had become your dwelling place? Something greater and more vast than all of that desert that went on and on forever all around us, greater and even more vast than all of that sky under which you patiently awaited the appearance of something that would fill you with joy and then send you back into the world with a smile on your lips. But some philosophers have a poet's soul that could not conceive of you being able to walk forward, your gaze held aloft and a smile on your lips, toward the center of this esplanade, without it corresponding to something greater than a center . . . for this center to be nothing more than the random final point of a trajectory that is just as random, that of a life in which the events are neither more nor less organized than a fistful of stones thrown with your eyes closed and that, maybe, the unfolding of our lives is made up of nothing more than a series of coincidences much greater than our feeble wills. But your executioner has nothing of a poet or a philosopher about him, he brutally pushes you to keep you moving toward your final destination and the heavy chains that hamper your steps nearly send you falling . . . and, as your body stumbles forward, something seems to hold you by the shoulders . . . you lower your head and resume your march toward that unexpected center from where you will rise up from among us. Or maybe not. Who is to say?

Still burning from what Nadine had failed to see in me, by which I mean anything at all, I hadn't looked on the whole situation favorably, a situation that had seemed to me no more and no less than a scam . . . that Stan had leapt at the opportunity to possess, for very little cost, a kind of general handyman, a deluxe slave, one who would serve him by maintaining his garden, of course, but also by cleaning the house, repairing odds and ends, doing the shopping, running administrative errands, and above all, by making him look important in front of his compatriots, who only possessed poor, needy help from the Philippines, Pakistan, or Afghanistan, when he introduced Mansour, his landscape architect . . . I would have preferred that Mansour return to Damascus to be among his own, his family. I tried hard, and on several occasions, to make him see reason . . . But what was left to him of reason at this point? I also asked our employer to assist me in this aim by returning his passport to him, but he refused, alluding to a "temporary burnout" and stating that things would eventually go back to normal. I then contacted his family, appealing to them for a repatriation for medical reasons, but it proved to be impossible, on their end, to obtain a visa and come to Saudi Arabia to get him out of there . . . I even tried to get assistance from our embassy, but they were all, and quite justly, occupied with other matters that were much more serious than the repatriation of a fellow citizen who had been suddenly transformed into an ass. As I was leaving the Syrian Embassy, I looked over at the Embassy of France, which adjoined it, wondering if perhaps they could come to our aid in the name of human rights and our love of the French language and yet, very quickly, the memory of my last soirée dispelled any hope. Distress leading to even crazier ideas, as it often does, I had even considered slipping us in, Mansour and me, via the underground passage that connected the gardens of the French Embassy to the courtyard of the residence of the Ambassador of Algeria . . . the dickhead from Cultural Services had told me in confidence, shortly before the drunken disaster that had ruined our friendship, that a secret tunnel had been constructed in case of emergency so as to permit the Algerian Ambassador and the members of his family to take flight "via" France . . . and so I imagined us, dust-covered in the middle of the salon belonging to His Excellency the Algerian Ambassador, requesting asylum and protection for the great-great-grandson of their nation's founder . . . but that scenario, for some strange reason, seemed pretty dicey, and this is how Mansour soon found himself a prisoner of Stan and Nadine, of the Kingdom of Saudi Arabia, and of himself.

That is everything I had come to believe, at least initially. That my friend, convinced that he was a donkey, had become the slave of a pretentious and Machiavellian couple . . . but, as time passed, a new image of Stan and Nadine materialized, and of the whole situation, in a manner that was unexpected and quite surprising, to say the least. I was still welcome to visit Mansour, to speak to him, to take him out, to go for a spin in his beautiful red Camaro or drive him out into the desert. Stan seemed to often be absent, leaving very early and coming home very late, he ran into Mansour fairly infrequently and Nadine fairly infrequently as well, it seemed to me. On the rare occasions that I saw him, he was wandering between his office and the kitchen, as if the captive of some enchantment, blurting out an asshole or a fuck along the way, quite innocently, then disappearing for good into a bedroom that I eventually figured out was his own . . . I also understood that Mansour spent the large part of his day, if not the entire day, in a bedroom that belonged to Nadine. All hope crushed, sick from jealousy, I still sought, with a heavy heart, to find out what they were doing in that bedroom. Reading and talking, replied Mansour, plainly and without irony . . . even as if, and again, this was over the course of many days, this was some sort of self-evident fact . . . as if there was nothing else that could take place in that bedroom, beyond reading and talking. But I didn't believe a word of it . . . without thinking that Mansour had lied to me, I had begun to believe he no longer had sound enough judgment to know that fucking was not a part of the elementary rules of cordiality. As the days went by, both of them maintained this strange rapport, this practically adulterous daily life . . . He, the patient, and her, the healer who dispensed the treatments that were best suited to his enfeebled state within an atmosphere of sensuality that wasn't the least bit appropriate . . . as if he was the sick son and she the attentive mother. I pictured her, stretched out on her bed, naked or practically naked, as Mansour had confided to me, and him sitting directly on the floor to listen to her talk and read aloud from all kinds of books . . . A lot of poetry, and it's doing me a world of good, the poetry! She can do that while she reads poetry? I secretly asked myself as I made my way into the conjugal bedroom to fetch him and take him for a spin in the desert, seeing her effectively half-naked, stretched out on her stomach, her index finger tracing the lines of an open book, a see-through shawl carelessly covering her back and her ass, and indeed, reciting aloud the verses of Hafiz or Khayyám to the donkey that Mansour had become, at the foot of her bed like one would have a pet, or a slave, or a kind of eunuch from whom someone had distractedly neglected to snip off the threatening bits . . . and I couldn't bring myself to picture anything else, as I accompanied him to the top of his dune, than what imposed itself on me with force and violence . . . and while Mansour saw whatever it was he was able to see out there beyond the dunes, I struggled with the onslaught of stills from the film that was being played out before my eyes, as if they had been there, right in front of me . . . both of them naked in that bed, in that bedroom in which clouds of incense and oud continually floated among the stacks of books scattered here and there and her, kneeling, in the middle of the bed . . . her head thrown back and her mouth open and her neck extended, from which, at the end of a silver chain, was suspended a cross, hanging over an open book out of which she declaimed, aloud and intended for the ass that was buttressed behind her, the poetry of Khayyám or Adonis or Hafiz or whomever else it might be . . . until it turned to cries! While the ass sunk himself in deeply, slow and deep, she asked while she still could of the animal that had climbed up behind her as if it was feeding time and the fodder had to be quickly swallowed down, an eye wide open and trained on the bedroom door and fearing, like a frightened animal, that his food would be unjustly taken away or that his head would be cut off . . . while she stretched out while she splayed out while she spread as wide as possible so he could enter even farther, even deeper, she asked him again, head thrown back, eyes already closed, mouth open wide and neck extended with its silver chain from the end of which a cross stirred and swung and waved . . . while the animal grabbed hold of her body with its entire body and glued its skin against hers while it nuzzled its muzzle in a manner of speaking into her scented curls and keeping a fearful eye on the door and abruptly holding his hand across Nadine's mouth so as to disappear, the two of them, through moans and stifled cries . . .

While Stan was fermenting his wine in his bathroom, in the company of his memories or what remained of them thanks to his regular consumption of that shit, which he drank without allowing it enough time to settle or mature as it passed through the alembics he had fashioned and that could have been made by any ten-year-old kid . . . sometimes even consuming it directly from the bathtub, a red, nearly black liquid that reeked of alcohol and that went directly, without even stopping by his stomach, to muddle his brain and erase any memory that might explain his presence in Saudi Arabia, his marriage to Nadine, his having gone to live among the Arabs . . . not even remembering anymore that he had once, at a certain time in his life, wanted to discover something more than his miserable suburb, that he had at one time hoped to discover the magic of the Orient and that he had thought he had found that magic, and rightly so, concentrated within the person of Nadine . . . but also found the loss of nearly all of his reason, which left him at the edge of the bathtub, cursing away at all the assholes who crossed his life's path and most definitely not getting anything about anything . . . having become, thanks to drinking that homemade shit, worse off than Mansour, Stan could no longer understand anything whatsoever about the trajectory that his life had been following, a shitty one, really, and of which the outcome was in little doubt to any conscious onlooker. Death in the land of the Arabs, one way or another . . . Dead drunk at the edge of the bathtub while Nadine and Mansour, upstairs, gradually returning to reality, short of breath and their sight still blurred from the flashes of pleasure that took their time fading but returning all the same to that sad, tragic reality, of which I couldn't quite yet see all of the angles, and with regard to which I still harbored a certain sense of suspicion, a certain skepticism, when Mansour, atop his dune, told me that Nadine knew how to empty him of everything that weighed upon him, that she could return to him his empty gaze, face leaned over the void, open hands draped across her legs . . . whereas I thought that this was nothing but a vulgar attempt to cover their tracks, to divert me from that which had taken hold inside of me as far as certainty and anguish . . . even as Mansour continued to feed me his nonsense . . . his head rested on Nadine's thighs so as to find peace, like a hundred and fifty years earlier, when Léon Roches rested his own torment-filled head upon Abdelkader's legs so that he would heal him of his pain and so he could drift off to sleep with his heart at peace only to wake up in the middle of the night and discover Abdelkader in a state of rapture . . . Léon Roches, that complicated figure of the nineteenth century, at once Abdelkader's translator and his secretary, confidant and spy, perhaps friend and perhaps traitor, who felt it crucial to bear witness: *I succeeded with great difficulty in extricating myself from that mound of mud, stones, and corpses, and I arrived in Abdelkader's tent in a deplorable state. My burnoose and my haik were soiled. In a word, I explained what had just happened to me. Abdelkader had me supplied with other clothing and I went to sit next to him. I was under the influence of a nervous excitation that I could not master. Heal me, I said to him, heal me or I would rather die, for in this state I feel I am incapable of serving you. He calmed me, had me drink an infusion of schiehh and placed my head, which I could no longer support, on one of his knees. He was crouching in the Arab fashion; I was stretched out beside him. He placed his hands on my head, which he had removed from the haik and the chechias, and under his gentle touch it was not long before I was asleep. I awoke well on into the night; I opened my eyes and I felt comforted. The smoky wick of an Arab lamp barely illuminated the emir's great tent. He was upright on his feet, three steps away from me; he thought me asleep. Both his arms, raised up to the height of his head, lifting from both sides his burnoose and his haik, which were of a milky whiteness, and fell in splendid folds. His beautiful blue eyes, lined with black lashes, were raised up, and his lips, slightly parted, seemed to still be reciting a prayer even though they were unmoving. He had reached a state of ecstasy. His aspirations toward the heavens were such that he no longer seemed to touch the ground.*

6.

In commemoration of the fortieth anniversary of the death of the Saudi king Faisal, the newspaper *Al Jazeera* had thought it markedly symbolic to run a headline about the speech the king had given to the United Nations, along with his portrait, and the obvious caption "A King's Speech!" I scanned through the main points of the editorial while enjoying my coffee on the terrace of the Starbucks at the Royal Mall, where I had actually found the paper and in which I was reading the traditional intimations of the grandeur of the House of Saud and the traditional incitations to a surge of pride among the Arab people and the entire Muslim community. As for me, I was markedly struck by Faisal's gaze and by its resemblance to that of Mansour and that of Abdelkader. All three shared a very slightly cross-eyed look that conferred upon them something haughty, sublime, gentle, and disconcerting all at once. A look that projected me back in time to my childhood in Damascus, in the 1980s, in the days when we were taught love and pride

for the nation, and sometimes for Arab civilization, and where
the phrase "remember the tears of King Faisal" had in some
way become a popular expression, almost a proverb destined for
anyone who was feeling sorry for their lot in life . . . and as for
the phrase "even kings shed tears," this, in turn, was made use
of when consoling young boys who were ashamed not to have
quite grown up yet. "Remember the tears of King Faisal" had
become, in the Syria of my youth, an admonition intended to
make men of us. At the office, I couldn't resist the impulse to
search the web for King Faisal's famous speech, during which
his voice had cracked into a thousand pieces before the cameras
of the entire world. Several links proposed, under headings such
as "The King's Speech" or "The Speech of the Last King" or
even "The Last King of the Arabs," to stream the video, in black
and white and in poor quality but in which it was possible to
see King Faisal's troubled face and hear his equally troubled
voice: *My brothers, what are we waiting for? For the world's conscience
to rise by itself? Where is this world's conscience? The great mosque of
Jerusalem is calling for you to rescue it and save it . . . To save it from
its suffering and its humiliation! What are we waiting for? What is it
that holds us back? Are we frightened of death?*

I paced around the office like a caged animal. In circles.
Something was stirring in the bottom of my stomach, something urgent and infuriating that prevented me from concen-
trating on my work. Nadine's face appeared to me, insistent, in
the reflection on my computer screen or on that of the window in front of which I isolated myself and outside of which
Riyadh's heartbeat continued to thump away. I chased away the
image of Nadine, and the heavy wave of desire that came with
it, by remembering our years spent at the French high school
in Damascus, where Mansour and I had become inseparable . . .

spending the majority of our time deep in discussion, in the back of the classroom or a corner of the schoolyard, about politics and about religion, but also wondering, together, if Faisal had or had not been a good king, if the trembling of his voice hadn't been fake and if his tears hadn't been theatrical and if his outbursts of rage had been no more than political acumen . . . We had the facts and knew how things appeared on the surface, and we attempted to see in behind them, to separate the real from the false and to bring the realest of the real out into the light . . . *Oh my brothers . . . please forgive my emotion . . . if my voice trembles, if I tremble before you . . . but when I see our sacred sites profaned, defiled, trespassed upon . . . I ask God with all sincerity, if he has not destined me for jihad, to not leave me among the living for one more instant!* And despite his Islamic emphases and his at times simplistic nationalism, nothing could diminish the admiration that we reserved for him or the influence of his gaze.

Mansour had religiously told me the story of his great-great-grandfather and, even if it sometimes bored me, I listened just as religiously . . . as if there was something sacred about it and as if it was, at least in part, the story of my country. For hours on end, during which we could wander, without even quite knowing how, from the story of Abdelkader to a scientific question. Innocent and quite excited to discover the powers of our minds, the pleasures of reasoning, we dove without restraint into the vast seas of algebra, of geometry, of physics and astronomy, without restraint and without any fear of drowning as we attempted to solve equations that were far too complex at our age and without concern about getting lost as we attempted to imagine the galactic clusters that danced through the infiniteness of the universe . . . Those beautiful discussions, which often lasted hours and sometimes entire nights, they bore a resemblance, all things considered, to those Abdelkader may have engaged in, in Pau, with Bishop Dupuch and General Daumas. Discussions that touched on everything and in particular on mathematics, not for a particular use but to develop a spirit of reflection and to balance, even to harmonize, the two ways of understanding: a rational way and an intuitive way . . . so that thought could advance on two legs, or so they said. The three of them in the genteel salon of a castle in Pau, trying to solve Zeno's mysterious paradox, repeatedly trying to catch a glimpse of the solution only to have it escape them once again, physically, even, because Abdelkader held out his arm toward Daumas, or perhaps toward Bishop Dupuch, explaining that he still needed to reach across half of the distance to touch his friend's shoulder and half again of that distance and half again of that half and so forth right up until Abdelkader's hand, his fingers were infinitely close to Daumas's shoulder, close enough to feel the warmth and then the agitation and finally the substance . . . perhaps alluding to Descartes on the one hand and to al-Khwarizmi on the other in order to understand why Abdelkader's hand ended up reaching the shoulder of Daumas . . . and it was through that word, perhaps uttered at that exact moment—infinitely—that they had all felt, all three of them, that only a passage through the infinite could explain that Abdelkader's hand had indeed ended up touching Daumas's shoulder . . . or perhaps that word was never uttered and they had had nothing but dubious, erroneous, absurd explanations . . . Either way! The very act of trying to understand and to solve such a heavy mathematical problem could do nothing less than elevate them, improve them, and bring to them nobility and ease when it came to resolving much more concrete and everyday questions . . . and perhaps Abdelkader thought back with affection on those long discussions in the castle, discussions that nourished their friendship and fed the benevolence and the admiration of the people of Pau then Bordeaux then Amboise then Paris . . . perhaps he remembered this in his corner of the great Umayyad Mosque even as, at that same moment, perhaps at precisely that moment, in Algiers, Henri Poincaré, while he gave his lecture on light cones, his talk on the new mathematics of his time, quadratic forms and non-Euclidian geometry . . . having interrupted his conference for a moment to collect himself or the thread of his reasoning . . . perhaps for a moment, turning his head toward the large window of the amphitheater of the university in Algiers and catching a glimpse, in the distance, of the Moorish houses, perhaps he spared a thought for Abdelkader and a smile for the long drawing room discussions that had often ended in laughter but that bore witness, at least, to the spiritual and intellectual vitality of those final years of the nineteenth century . . . or maybe not, maybe Henri Poincaré was only thinking, during that short breather in the middle of his long explanation, of his wedding that was to take place four days later . . .

This crowd that separates me from you is infinite.

From the terrace of the Starbucks at Al Faisaliyah Center, a sort of futurist pyramid that forms an axis with the Kingdom Tower, I watched, and not without trepidation—or was it contempt? or maybe it was disgust? or simply a failure to understand?—the comings and goings of the people between those two monuments . . . a flood that flowed the length of Olaya Street in taxis or luxury 4-x-4s and poured forth in swarms of women in black and men in white, all rushing forward, albeit nonchalantly, into the two multi-use complexes to spend or earn their money. The noonday heat had left me isolated on the terrace and had sent the few other customers running for the café's interior and the cool of the air conditioning. A dry and burning heat that added to the feeling of trepidation that had come over me and that kept me company through the duration of my lunch break. How was it possible for us to live in such conditions? Under that oven-like heat, scurrying like rats to take refuge in the frozen galleries of shopping malls to frantically purchase all manner of pointless objects that we then make absolutely indispensable . . . alarmed to notice that the only mechanism to have endured since the golden age of Baghdad or Damascus was that of the souks and the market stalls . . . transformed these days into glittering buildings and luxury signs with, all around them, the throng of unskilled workers whose job it was to maintain the city's artificial shine. Perhaps this is the Arab people to whom Faisal had been calling, the rich people and the millions of poor people who live only to become rich, that's the incoming tide, with, transversely, the thousands of poor people who are convinced that they will never be rich people and who want to blow it all up, and the hundreds of rich people who subsidize this desperate initiative in case it one day becomes profitable . . . *Where are you, people of Arabia?* shouted King Faisal on the television, on the radio, with the trembling voice of a little girl and tears of incomprehension, to nations too busy making money or too busy dreaming about making it. This is all we have retained of the grandeur of our civilization . . . souks full of overflowing stalls! And I unreservedly included myself in this dark tableau since I was taking a break on the Starbucks terrace before returning to the office to draw up plans for the new buildings that we would soon be erecting in the city of Riyadh. This is where we had ended up, the Arab peoples that Faisal's big eyes had sought out before the cameras of the entire world. What good had come of the great thoughts of our philosophers? I asked myself, still sitting in the hell that was that terrace, to which the Starbucks servers no longer even dared to venture . . . sitting there roasting, boiling, and thinking about those two, Nadine and Mansour, who were miraculously escaping from the natural course of things . . . By loving each other . . . my God, by loving each other . . . while I sat shivering in the dry noonday heat, in the middle of a deserted terrace. I was able to make out the sound that the sun was pulling from the branches of the poor palm trees lined up along the side of the avenue . . . a shiver. This is where we had ended up, and we were taking part in the *Nahda*, the renaissance of the great Arab-Muslim civilization, upon which King Faisal called with all his hopes for the liberation of Palestine . . . here, to spend and to make money, under a debilitating sun and surrounded by the hum of the grieving palm trees. Maybe because everything had become too complicated for us to understand . . . impossible to understand, and Ibn Sina himself, in that universe of knowledge that would have required the longevity of Abraham or of Noah to be able to produce a synthesis of it all and to understand what connected one problem to the others . . . Ibn Sina himself, if he were permitted to return from the dead, would immediately turn around and return among them or would make some cash and then spend it frantically at Zara or Swarovski.

This insurmountable world that separates us.

Or, Faisal's tears were no more than an avowal of his impotence when faced with what was being woven discreetly but powerfully before his eyes, that backward and violent religious practice inherited from 'Abd al-Wahhab and Ibn Hanbal. Were Faisal's tears those of a prisoner? He would have wanted to exhibit a look so full of ardor that the light of his eyes would unify the crowds into a single man who could shine the dignity and grandeur of the Arabs back onto the world, but instead unexpected tears sprang forth and his voice cracked, reminding him before the cameras of the entire world that he was a prisoner to himself, because he was the emblematic heir, the noble protector, the guarantor by blood of the dark side of Islam that no mind or spirit, no matter how great, could ever illuminate. Faisal's eyes may have revealed, before the cameras of the entire world, the end of a civilization.

And it was perhaps also to cries of *Gassouh! Gassouh!* that the great minds had gathered before the fortress of al-Ma'mun with al-Kindi or al-Khwarizmi at their head, chanting at the top of their lungs, *Gassouh! Gassouh!* so that their beloved caliph would cut short his decision on the case of Ibn Hanbal so that no trace of that retrograde perspective remained, or so they thought at the time, simplistic and binary, or so they thought already, such that it would be possible to go on reflecting peacefully between the walls of the house of wisdom, such that it would be possible to continue serenely transcribing and annotating the ponderous pages of Aristotle, Plato, and Plotinus, and to serenely let the long process of mutating Greek and Latin letters into Arabic letters take its own course . . . So that Baghdad might continue its influence over that entire region thus pacified, prosperous, and drawing toward it all the intellect of humanity, whether it was from Persia, India, or China . . . So that Baghdad might continue to be, they must have then thought, the womb of a new humanity . . . So that Baghdad might continue to be Baghdad. Or maybe not. Who is to say? Al-Kindi and al-Khwarizmi, too busy solving their equations, had not responded to the call of the crowd and had perhaps downplayed the words of Ibn Hanbal in considering, erroneously, that an elementary thought, simplified, dark, would inevitably have no power in that radiant Baghdad . . . erroneously, for it to end up there, in that hall of the United Nations where the entire world's press awaited the arrival of King Faisal, to hear what he had had to say about Jerusalem or his calls for the *Nahda* of the Arab peoples . . . in that antechamber of the United Nations where Faisal's voice had broken into a million pieces and where his tears hadn't flowed solely to save Jerusalem . . . readjusting his white *shemagh* and his gold-embroidered cape while the eyes of the entire world were trained on his own, emphasized by thick and angular brows . . . while the eyes of the entire world were focused on his face, the face of a royal eagle, stately, penetrating, aquiline . . . during that moment of silence, readjusting his white *shemagh* and his cape and perhaps realizing his error, before shattering on the screens of the entire world . . . during that moment of silence, still maintaining the appearance of an invincible warrior, until he broke down in tears . . . *What are we waiting for? What is it that holds us back? Are we frightened of death?*

. . . An error in judgment like a simple calculation error? Who is to say? And would it even be useful to know, today, while everyone is shouting *Gassouh! Gassouh!* like a doleful song to accompany Mansour in his slow procession toward the center of that square of purity where he will be purified, they think, as if he will be liberated from some evil . . . from evil itself . . . And those men who sing . . . and my God how they sing! . . . to be purified as well through Mansour's passion. *History is also made of all that we do not say*, asserted Ibn Khaldun as he relativized the contributions of the great caliphs . . . Well of course! What was growing among the people? What were the bonds that united them? What ambition drove them into Ibn Hanbal's arms? . . . despite Caliph Faisal's invincible appearance, his dense eyebrows framing his intense gaze, despite his tears and his voice in a thousand pieces but continuing to appeal to the renaissance, to the grandeur . . . What was it that kept the people in Ibn Hanbal's arms? Who is to say, my God? Who is to say? *History is an art where the wise and the ignorant find themselves on the same level,* said that same Ibn Khaldun as well . . . and what he very well could have said right here, in my place and with my ignorant voice, watching Mansour advance laboriously toward what is supposed to be the center of the square and the center of humanity and the center of the universe.

And so I close my eyes to no longer hear their cries. I let my voice resonate inside my head, telling myself that history is being made right here and now, through the energy of those in this entranced crowd, by this crowd gathered and bound together in this state of inebriation that it will abandon once Mansour is divided in two but which it will remember and which it will want to live over the same old way it lives, breathes, exists . . . like something essential and vital that no witness will inscribe in the annals of history as being notable, significant, foundational . . . and no one will know anything of Mansour or of the role he played in history. And yet Mansour advances in a straight line . . . he moves forward with his eyes held high. Mansour, you are the most beautiful of the stoics! You have the grandeur of Marcus Aurelius and the humility of Epictetus! You are the lord we sacrifice for a new world! And yet nobody will remember your name, Mansour, nobody . . . You are the last man of a civilization. After you, Mansour, mankind will scatter into savage hordes to destroy Palmyra, Damascus, and even Medina . . . into savage hordes to burn everything that the Arab mind has been able to establish as the jewels of knowledge . . . After you, Mansour, black and savage hordes will ride about in luxury 4x4s and roam the sterile deserts to raze entire cities and erect new ones, adorned with glittering buildings and verdant parks and improbable lakes . . . but which will be, in reality, new sterile deserts . . . vulgar mirages. After you, Mansour, no more Arabs! You are the last of the Arabs. Even I, Mansour, I will forget you as everyone else was able to forget King Faisal's tears, and I will ride about in the back of a pickup across seas of sand crying *Gassouh! Gassouh!* just to live, Mansour, just to keep on living.

Or else I was mistaken, full of bitterness in front of my Starbucks coffee, thinking evil thoughts before the back and forth of all of that money circulating between Faisaliyah and Kingdom Tower . . . perhaps the souks and the stalls, in their abundance, were the path required for the Arab-Muslim renaissance that King Faisal called for . . . but it would take time and a lot of patience and most likely some selflessness and maybe even some abjuration for him to see that renaissance with his own eyes. Because it probably wouldn't see the day for another fifty years or maybe even for a century or two . . . the time it would take for us to overdose on yogurt, on clothes and on cars . . . for other needs to emerge, spiritual and intellectual this time . . . What a mess, my God! Who is to say? Or maybe nothing will be left of this civilization, each region will turn back to its own distant and less controversial beginnings and attempt to formulate a new identity . . . if so, I will become a Mesopotamian . . . The Phoenician Lebanese, the Egyptian, they will handily find a way to converse and to write in the language of the pharaohs, the Maghrebi will reestablish his Berber identity by making a clean break with his frustrated Arabness and Emir Abdelkader will be perceived, by some, as an Arab invader who ended up falling in with the French and betraying the earth that had welcomed his ancestors . . . The statues of him will be destroyed and he will be buried once and for all among all of those to whom he said he was the heir, Ibn 'Arabi, Ibn Sina . . . What a mess! All that will remain of the Arabs will be these mega-urbanized tribes between the Hejaz and the eastern region of the peninsula by way of the Najd . . . and still . . . some differentiate themselves from others for strategic reasons, political, economic . . . What an incomprehensible mess!

Perhaps you're actually nothing more than an ass that we sacrifice in order to be able to understand something of this world.

Abdelkader, astride his black stallion, his drinker of winds, was pounding across the plains of the Tafna in the middle of which, perhaps, he abruptly came to a halt, as if someone had called to him. He turned around and saw, perhaps, in the stares of his men, determination and joy even though their destination, which is to say gunshots screams blood death, ought to have instead engendered stares filled with concern and solemnity. So perhaps Abdelkader dismounted his majestic black horse and he ordered his men to do the same, and perhaps he decided to interrupt for a moment the momentum of that charge which was to be resolved at the first village or the first encampment they found on their trajectory and inevitably had to be resolved, as expected as appointed as foreseen, in the din of gunshots and screams, in the smell of gunpowder and blood, among the lamentations of the women and the silence of death . . . perhaps right then, Abdelkader decided it ought to be otherwise, which is to say not so much in its form because it couldn't begin other than in screams and couldn't end other than in silence . . . otherwise, then, and he had his men get down off their mounts, asked them to sit in circles around him, had them recite prayers and, perhaps, to go even further than prayers, bid them to take refuge within themselves and to go off in search of the reasons for their fight and the source of their religion so that, as he often said, the Muslim not be in protest against Islam . . . and perhaps he went even further by asking them to try to see the beauty in that coarse and stony plain which surely had the look of a desert of stones and dust that spread out endlessly around them and maybe he went even further by tracing for them the great paths of those in whose footsteps he faithfully followed . . . traced and bequeathed across the centuries, by his father and his father's father and by 'Abd al-Qadir al-Jilani and by Ibn 'Arabi, his great master, and by Ibn Sina as well and by Husayn ibn Mansur al-Hallaj, indeed by Suhrawardi as well, and by Muhammad of course, and by all of those who had seen the desert and who had wanted to trace their trajectories in its sand . . . and just as certainly mentioning Isa, Musa, and Ibrahim . . . as well as those who had maybe never seen the desert but who had sensed it all the same and thus mentioning Plotinus, Aristotle, and the divine Plato . . . Who knows what Emir Abdelkader may have said to his men during those breaks, in their circles . . . who knows how Abdelkader transformed those circular positions into vertical ascensions? Worry-provoking positions for the traitor's encampments or for Bugeaud's ranks, who wondered as to the significance of the warriors waiting, seated in their circles around their leader, or their master, really, he too perhaps sitting with his eyes closed, tirelessly recounting to his men not a synthesis of the thought of the divine Plato or Plotinus or Ibn Sina . . . but simply their names so that, should they be victorious, they would simply be saved from the obscurity of forgetfulness . . . so that those names themselves should be bequeathed . . . and suffice it to say that while they fought among the stones and the sand, while they struggled in the wind and the dust . . .

suffice it to say that they fought so that the thought of Aristotle the first master and that of Averroes the second master might live on . . . among the stones the sand the wind and the Arabs . . . Then perhaps he rose up majestically from among his men, at the end of a prayer or at the end of an explanation, and he leapt up nobly on his mount and proudly drew his saber from its sheath and launched the attack in the name of God but also in the name of Muhammad and of his daughter Fatimah and of her husband the Imam ʿAli as well as in the name of all those who had brought life to Islam and made it grow, which is to say in the name of Ibn ʿArabi in the name of al-Farabi of Ibn Sina of Ibn Rushd of Ibn Khaldun . . . launched the attack while crying out all of those names to the surprised but admiring stare of General Bugeaud . . . And even, on occasion, going one against ten versus the tribes of traitors or the ranks of the French king's soldiers, who were mystified and dumbfounded to hear amid the deafening clamor of cannonblasts and gunshots and swordstrokes . . . to hear amid the clamor of war all those names but also those of Aristotle of Plotinus and of the divine Plato and even that of Jesus, as if those warriors from another world were defending, in the name of Islam, humanity in its entirety. And that plain transformed itself into a vast battlefield upon which the horsemen, dressed in simple cowls of white or brown wool, charged from every direction against the King of France's elegant soldiers . . . elegant soldiers who were surprised to see, at the last minute, these ghostly horsemen spring at them . . . surprised to see, at the last minute, sabers being raised into a sky full of dust and surprised, finally, to feel their throats cut.

On the long, stony, and arid plains of the Tafna, which perhaps he saw as great pastures, Abdelkader had his mount rear up like a flash with the famous lines of Ibn ʿArabi in his mind:

لقد صار قلبي قابلا كل صورة   فمرعى لغزلان ودير لرهبان

وبيت لأوثان وكعبة طائف   وألواح توراة ومصحف قرآن

أدين بدين الحب أنى توجهت   ركائبه فالحب ديني وإيماني

My heart has become able to take on all forms
It is a pasture for gazelles and an abbey for monks
It is a temple for idols and the Kaaba for any to circle around it
It is the tables of the Torah and also the tomes of the Qur'an
The religion I practice is that of love
Wherever its mounts may turn, love is my religion and my faith!

and sensing, perhaps, for the duration of that flash during which his mount reared up and he brandished his saber just before bringing it down on the neck of one of the elegant soldiers of the King of France, sensing that the fleetingness of this scene would be fixed in bronze, here and there, in that new nation they would call Algeria, and sensing—or maybe more than sensing, maybe seeing . . . seeing beyond the decades and the centuries . . . seeing the bronze statues desecrated, here and there, in that old country that would continue to be called Algeria, covered in obscene writing, in insults, in spit and in piss—seeing perhaps, during the time his horse was reared up and kicking and bounding forth, that all peoples who lose a thought, a grandeur, are inevitably bounding forth into violence and self-destruction.

When the blade is brought down on your neck, an entire people, an entire nation, an entire community of believers, will return to a pre-Islamic period, dark, violent, apocalyptic.

I left the scorching terrace of Al Faisaliyah and the pessimism that it had inspired in me and I raced over to Stan and Nadine's house to find Mansour and remind him about

Abdelkader's circles and Faisal's tears in the hope that something would come of it or that something would cease happening in his donkey head and that everything would return to the place it was destined to be . . . our lives, their trajectories . . . and to make him catch at least a glimpse of the possibility of holding onto something from Abdelkader's circles, from Faisal's tears, of holding onto something of this world that was evolving so quickly or, if absolutely necessary, to just accept the monstrosity and to settle for understanding even a tiny little part of it, one that was a more appropriate size for us, and if absolutely necessary to give up on that which is too big for us and to at long last make a fresh start on a new existence devoid of pretention, without great aspirations, those the wide avenues of Riyadh bid us to pursue, from mall to mall, in luxury automobiles without worrying about the rest, about what isn't working or what we don't understand, and to hold on to the small pleasures stolen here and there, as we had so well begun to do, out among the cliffs of the Najd or in the bars of Dubai or the brothels of Manama, and then, even if the small pleasures turned out to be ephemeral, the tears would be just as brief. Full of hope in the luxurious Camaro as it flew through the deserted avenues of Riyadh, crushed by the sun at the height of that sweltering afternoon, full of hope that everything would return to how it had been before, I crossed that hell with a smile on my lips, between the rows of buildings packed one against another as if they were melted or soldered to that dry and hard earth where not a soul would dare take their shadow for a stroll and as if finally there were none left, no souls and no shadows . . . flying, with the sensation of being free and happy, inside the leather and air-conditioned interior of the luxurious Camaro, crossing that capital which had abruptly become Sodom or Gomorrah with the sensation of being reborn and of starting over . . . crossing Riyadh without ever encountering anyone other than King Abdullah and his welcoming face on the giant billboards that punctuated the length of Tahlia Street that I traveled down at top speed and right to its end until I was gobbled up by the streets, then the alleys that would lead us, my hope and me, to reclaim Mansour . . . And it was full of this hope that I stretched out my arm and that, miraculously once again, my finger reached the button of the intercom and I heard the bell ring in Stan and Nadine's villa . . .

7.

. . . AND NADINE'S VOICE, nearly unrecognizable through the intercom, informed me that Mansour wasn't there and that she was alone and would be glad if I came in for a moment. Even though I had made up my mind to convince everyone it was still possible to return to normal life, as I faced Nadine I found myself petrified, as if by Medusa, turned to stone by her beauty . . . I remained mute at the bottom of the stairs, which she descended to join me, mute as she took my arm to lead me out under the acacia, which, although it offered only slight shade, was still lifesaving beneath the violent sun that was starting to burn our skin. Mute as she rested her hand on my arm even though we were already in the dappled shade of that poor acacia and as she revealed to me that, in spite of everything, she couldn't do without this oppressive heat and that this earth, as distressed as it was, was her own . . . and as if there was any need to argue about it—or maybe it was simply to make conversation?—she explained to me how she had ended up here—here, right next to me, I thought discretely—her hand still resting on my arm and my heart racing under the garden's poor acacia . . . while she told me of her life or the important parts of it, like her childhood in al-Khobar where her father had migrated to try to make his fortune in petroleum and her teenage years at the French school of Riyadh where her father had changed careers to become a salesman of luxury RVs . . . And, while she unpacked her life for me, or what had been its watershed moments, like her studies in Paris and her thesis on Bergson, I sought on her face the tiniest details that made Nadine such an irresistible woman, in her way of tucking her curls back behind her ears, her gaze that was successively sad and cold and benevolent and hopeless and loving and her lips, ample and full and slightly parted, promising to offer all of her sensuality and even more . . . until I forgot the reason I had come, concentrated on that irresistibly attractive face and those lips that shared with me the Lebanon of her holidays and her first loves and her first battles and her first losses only to return, after a smile and as I sought once again the tiniest details that made up what seemed to me to be perfect harmony, to that thesis at the Sorbonne on Bergson and mysticism, which had left her without energy and without her bearings and without money in a Paris full of liquor and misadventures and illness, from which her father had more or less exfiltrated her against her will and brought her back to Riyadh where he had become responsible for the administration of a sports complex and where she had met Stan, who had seemed to be the exact opposite of Bergson, which she had seen as a clear sign and hadn't hesitated a single moment to reply with a Yes! when he had asked her to share her life with him immediately after her father's expulsion from Saudi Arabia for reasons related to age and taxation and then there was nothing left but the sun in her life, its burns and its glare, violent and vital at the same time . . . and I decided to give in entirely, she said, to giving up. In the dry heat of the Riyadh nights, I found comfort for my waiting solely in the company of the poets and the prophets. And I awoke, every morning, beside that lengthy waiting . . . Nadine maintained the distance between the two of us through the chronological unfolding of her existence—or was she showing me the trajectory that had brought her to where she was, under that acacia?—that distance I could not manage to reduce and I contented myself with her hand on my arm and with hearing resonate in me the Yes! she had recently pronounced as I attempted to comprehend the harmonious order or the random distribution that made Nadine's face such a marvel, violent and vital at the same time . . . right up until the day where everything finally came together in the revelation I had at the end of that long period of waiting. Until the day that time contracted itself to such a point that it had to break into pieces. No before and no after . . . a rupture I resisted but to which I finally yielded and in the face of which I gathered up all of my *élan vital*, preparing to throw myself forward to embrace each and every part . . . but Nadine didn't leave me enough time because she took me in her arms and squeezed me very hard as she told me that soon she would have to leave this country and that everything that should happen would happen, and when I went to extricate myself from her arms to find enough space so that my lips could reach hers, the front gate began to scrape and swing open and warn us of Ikram's arrival. Nadine's arms pushed me away just like that and I took flight as if something had happened between us and without letting Ikram's gaze meet my own.

Then, Mansour, another hope was born in me and I lost the one I had of leading you back to the life that we had lived before, and I lost, before Nadine's immense eyes, the life that had been my own. Because I too, Mansour, I hoped for something greater than myself so I could go on living a life that wasn't that of an animal and because I wasn't going to be able to hold up long against the need to understand something about this world where the pleasures seem to lack substance and the tears are of perpetual anguish. And that's where we are today, under this yellow sky where the winds taper the clouds, giving them the appearance of ephemeral trajectories.

Set free, the two hundred and sixty horses of the beautiful red Camaro reared up, raising the front of the car as it charged along the straightaway of Mekkah Road, all the other vehicles moving aside at its passage, allowing me to fly toward the red dunes of the desert of the Najd. I stopped where we had always stopped and I climbed the dune atop which Mansour had customarily isolated himself and I isolated myself, in turn, among the sand and the scent of burnt wood. Quickly, the sky seemed to run from blue to black, revealing the uncountable quantity of stars tracing paths from either side of its expanse . . . the trajectories of which I tried to follow without the least bit of success. As night gradually set in, the blackness of the sky veered toward a kind of impure white . . . streaks of stars soiled the absolute darkness of the void. The chill then pushed me to regain the interior of the Camaro to contemplate the exterior in the sort of torpor characteristic of those who can bear no more . . . Nadine came back to me over and over, almost as present as if she had been there, right beside me, and I could marvel at her face and hear her irresistible call . . . as well as the strength of her voice and the warmth of her skin and the scent of her curls and the love of her eyes . . . In my dream, I gradually took Mansour's place behind Nadine's stretched-out, splayed-out, spread-wide body to go farther, go deeper, she asked me, head thrown back, eyes already closed, mouth open wide and neck extended, from which a silver cross stirred and swung and waved . . . and I thought I even cried out *I love you* in the heart of my fantasy. I lost consciousness lying beside Nadine, beside her beauty, her pleasure, and the streaks of stars that spurted all over the black that surrounded me and finally swallowed me up. A slight sunburn on my face woke me and when I opened my eyes, the raw light of the sun closed them for me immediately. I turned my head and got out of the car. I leaned against the trunk of the dust-covered Camaro, lit a cigarette, and contemplated the new day that was slowly spilling across the dunes. A whitish color spread across the sands and the rocks of the desert, giving it the look of a dead planet . . . the aftermath of an apocalypse. An unexplained anxiety grew within me as my eyes followed the serpentine meanderings of the path that led down to Mekkah Road. The freshness of the morning and the fatigue brought shivers to my body . . . and that anxiety won over me completely as the impression of being alone in the world carried me away. From afar, the still-empty Mekkah Road managed to convince me that Riyadh and the entire plateau of the Najd had been destroyed in the night . . . and maybe even worse . . . the planet destroyed in its entirety, without men and without the slightest trace of any kind of civilization . . . there was nothing left but me and the stone . . . me and the sand.

Look, Mansour, the sky is yellow! Why don't you raise your eyes up to the sky? What is the meaning behind that gaze of yours, unwavering and unfeeling, fixated on the unrelenting crowd that calls for your death? What is the sense of it, Mansour? What are you saying with your eyes, Mansour? Look,

Mansour, the sky is yellow . . . look at the sky, Mansour, it is made of beauty . . . look at the spirals drawn across it and the interlacing woven across it . . . look at the sky and go there! There is no longer any man worthy of your gaze, no longer any man who measures up to your eyes. What do you see, Mansour, among this crowd and these cries? Yes, what are you able to see a few feet away from the point where you will disappear? What are you still able to see as you guide yourself toward that pail and mat? Are they all you can see? I followed you and I climbed laboriously up that dune where you, Mansour, still rested, sitting lightly, and, while I continued to toil away, to sink into the goldenness of the sand, to struggle for breath, you offered up your gaze to me . . . What is the structure of this eternal world? I wanted to ask you when I saw that clarity in your eyes. Your empty gaze. Is it emptiness? What is it you see that is so great? What is it you see that is so great beyond the immensity that opens up before you? Beyond the dunes that unfold into infinity? Beyond the emptiness as far as the eye can see? Or had your gaze been full? Full of a density that was almost inhuman or maybe, quite the opposite, full of a density that was at the origins of what we are, at the origins of humankind. Between two things, as close as they may be, there is always a path that separates them and along that path other things are inevitably discovered . . . that's what your eyes told me while I was suffering on my way to join you and to come to your aid. But it's you, Mansour, or rather your eyes, Mansour, that pulled me from the sands that were holding me back.

I reentered Riyadh all dirty but without the slightest urge to stop by my place, freshen myself up, have something to eat, and even less of an urge to go to work and return to something that resembled everyday life . . . It was maybe 10 a.m. and I

meandered through the galleries of the Royal Mall as I waited . . .
as I waited for something to happen . . . as I waited for something inevitable to happen. Near the central roundabout, I once
again encountered little Aziadeh holding her father's hand, and
inevitably, I exchanged a smile with him. He let go of Aziadeh's
hand, who took off at full speed around the circumference of
the roundabout while swinging her arms . . . back to making
the helicopter or the airplane propeller. And then, inevitably
once again, our trajectories split away from one another. The
Starbucks had just opened, and I forced myself to go inside and
order a coffee and something to eat. With an eye still on the
exterior, I noticed that Aziadeh's father had sat down on the
same bench as the first time I had noticed him and that he once
again had that dazed look . . . which I must have had as well.
And maybe more than dazed, he bore a look of suffering, his
eyes hanging down with sadness and despair. It seemed as if we
were like two castaways who, in spite of ourselves, had survived
who knows what dreadful catastrophe or what horrible night-
mare, and had been delivered back to reality along the shores of
the glittering shops of the Royal Mall, which was just starting
to fill up . . . slowly . . . slowly . . . and I don't know what wave
carried me away only to set me back down next to him . . .
sitting side by side on that bench and the both of us watching
while Aziadeh turned endlessly around as I opened my mouth
and let it all out, all jumbled and in no semblance of order, but
absolutely all of it . . . without him being particularly amazed
or uncomfortable, not even surprised to hear me express myself
in French. He listened attentively, his gaze consistently sorrowful, to everything I had to say about Nadine, her face lit by
pleasure and her body stretched-out undressed and hanging
from Mansour's eyes, and Mansour's mind, or what remained

of it, his millions of neurons that were being transformed each day into grains of sand and the billions upon billions of grains of sand that formed the dune we went to each day so as to understand or at least try to understand something, without really getting into Abdelkader's story and Ibn 'Arabi's thought and what was afoot in the secret meetings at the embassy about the future of Syria and maybe of the entire Arab world and maybe even the whole world, period . . . and I'm not sure which wave carried the three of us away as I continued to let it all out as if yelling Help! Help! only for it to set us down around a table at the Starbucks where Aziadeh persisted in twisting the straw that the server had given her in every direction and I persisted in detailing in consistent disorder what seemed to me to be the facts and nothing but the facts . . . as exemplified by Zeno's paradox and Abdelkader's hand moving toward Bishop Dupuch's shoulder without ever reaching it and Mansour's head or what was left in it, as it was irreversibly transforming into the head of an ass that brayed behind Nadine's perfumed curls in that bedroom that smelled of oud or sandalwood where they recited the verse of Hafiz or Khayyám but also certainly that of Ibn 'Arabi, which was chanted aloud over the crumpled sheets of Nadine's bed . . . her voice, at once hoarse and hot and short of breath and straightaway supported by that of Mansour as he ceased his braying behind the perfumed curls of that exhausted body to take up the chanting . . . My God, the chanting . . . . picking up once more the verse of Ibn 'Arabi, on Nadine's heels, at the same spot where her voice had left off . . . in that Chamber of Love where the two of them had hidden away from everyone . . .

Leila has robbed me of my reason
O Leila, I said, have pity on the fallen

Her love is hidden away . . .
buried deep in entrails
O you alienated one, lift away the humiliation
I am lost and for her, a servant I have become

. . . while little Aziadeh, surprised, had begun to laugh and then to sing, behind my voice:

سلبت ليلى
مني العقل
قلت يا ليلى

إرحمي القتلى

حبها مكنون
في الحشا مخزون
أيها المفتون
قم بنا ذلا

. . . while her father continued to look at me without responding, full of sadness and despair, listening attentively as I let it all out and really anything at all so long as he took in, or at least so I was hoping, everything that was chewing away at my insides without finding an exit or a release or exploding and so that at last my entire head emptied itself of these shitty stories, that of Stan and his Westerns, the tears of King Faisal, the end of Arab civilization, maybe even Nadine's cries at the same exact moment I was letting all of this out, the acceleration of the beautiful red Camaro and the neglected thought of Ibn Sina, the misinterpreted thought of Ibn Rushd and the trampled-on thought of Ibn 'Arabi, the profaned statues of Abdelkader and François Hollande's smile . . . Outside, a wind picked up and pushed drifts of sand in through the glass-lined porticos of the Royal Mall. Grains rolled in unexpected ways across the shopping center's impeccable tiles. As if the earth was attempting something, a last stand. A losing battle, because as we all know, the earth included, not one drop of sand will be left in Riyadh in twenty or thirty more years. An army of cleaning operatives was deployed before our very eyes to erase, with blows of the scrub brush, the only thing that could remind us that we were in the middle of a desert . . . Aziadeh's father took advantage of this interruption to get to his feet and take over the dialog, telling me: You ought to put some order in your thoughts . . . order is always important when it comes to understanding . . . and that's precisely what you're hoping for . . . No? Take three thoughts, and by permutating them, that gives you six possible understandings . . . take five thoughts, one hundred and twenty-five possibilities! etc. He gathered up Aziadeh's hand and off they went, leaving me alone in front of the Starbucks table that the server had just cleaned with antibacterial spray, alone to calculate the possibilities of understanding for a thought that was based on even just ten concepts . . . Three million six hundred and twenty-eight thousand eight hundred! And I ended up telling myself that if it was understanding that we wanted, the slightest little bit, anything about anything at all, we would have to acquire the speed and the power of a computer . . . or maybe not, order having no importance at all, as if some sort of synthetic perception, a priori or a posteriori, was responsible for putting order into all thought . . . but who is to say? How are we to escape from the paradox of the eye that sees itself or the thought that thinks itself, or here, in this case, of the understanding that tries to understand itself . . . Lost in the jumble of knots making up these reflections and regretting that I hadn't brought up, during the entire time that I was confiding in the stranger of the Royal Mall, the critical view that the Muʿtazilites held about reason and knowledge, whether a priori or a posteriori, in the houses of wisdom of al-Ma'mun's flamboyant Baghdad . . . Lost in all those knots, I imagined Abdelkader lost in the interlacing of the friezes in the majestic Umayyad Mosque and perhaps he too, seeking to tally all of the possible permutations of the group of geometric transformations that were behind the implausible beauty of the ornamentation that hands, expert and skillful, had instinctively known how to deploy . . . trying to come up with a tally even as, perhaps at the same moment, in Algiers, Poincaré was knocking an audience flat on their asses by summarizing mathematics as a whole . . . I had forgotten to talk about that as well . . . thinking that I had told everything to that man, all jumbled and in no semblance of order . . . that I had revealed everything to that man, as if he would have been able to relieve my mind and been willing to make it his life's work. As she left, little Aziadeh turned back and shot me a look full of curiosity while I continued to perform my calculations in order to determine all of the possible variations surrounding the thinking of someone like Ibn ʿArabi or even Abdelkader and realizing that they would surpass, in number, a sky full of stars.

You can't see it, Mansour, but the crowd that demands you be put to death is black with hate. Blacker than a sky without stars. Without stars, without moon, and without God. What trajectory is it that has brought you all the way to the center of this esplanade? Was there only one and one alone? Or would any other path have unerringly brought you right here? Among all the possible combinations of fates, each one would have unerringly brought you right here. Here and now. Among all the possible trajectories, whether that of Nadine or Stan or the stranger of the Royal Mall, that of Ikram or my own . . . one alone brought you here. Yours. But I am convinced, Mansour, that all the others would have inevitably steered you to the center of this esplanade.

The stranger and his little girl had left me to my tallying the possible combinations of this thought or of that one. As I watched them leave, I asked myself if it was possible for even one single person to have existed who fully understood Ibn ʿArabi or Abdelkader or anybody at all . . . All things considered, perhaps the stranger had spoken correctly and had sent me off to founder in complete ignorance. I remembered Poincaré's texts on the foundations of knowledge. I remembered them with a touch of embarrassment, even shame . . . the embarrassment of having summoned all of those great men to my meager table at the Starbucks and the shame of having mixed them all up in this story . . . *For fifteen days,* wrote Poincaré, *every day I seated myself at my work table, stayed an hour or two, tried a great number of combinations and reached no results. One evening, contrary to my custom, I drank black coffee and could not sleep. Ideas rose in crowds; I felt them collide until pairs interlocked, so to speak, making a stable combination. By the next morning, I only had to write out the results.* A stable combination . . . and I conceded, disheartened, that all that remained was to once again give in to chance. Let all those ideas jostle around in my head, let them turn over, so to speak, until they result, or never do result, in a stable combination that would allow me to understand any part of this story . . .

An unexpected humidity had settled upon the city. The winds had turned. I arrived in Stan and Nadine's neighborhood, and as I got out of the Camaro, I was struck by a thick blanket of air that immediately glued itself to my face. The atmosphere, usually dry and stale, was laden with scents . . .

it seemed as if I could smell the wood of the row of tortuous acacias lining the street and it even seemed that the sounds of the city had found, via that air, a serendipitous conductor . . . the sounds of the cars, the hammer blows of the workers, the whistling of the blackbirds . . . I had almost believed myself to be in a city on the Mediterranean, Beirut or Algiers, and expected to catch a glimpse of the sea at any moment. Even the sound of the car door slamming resonated differently. I pushed open the gate and made my way into the grounds of the villa. Ikram's 4x4 wasn't there and I thought that maybe they had all gone out, forgetting to shut the gate behind them. I noticed that the garden had miraculously healed from its burns, had been tidied, cleared of the scrub that had choked it. They had even planted graceful blue hydrangeas to conceal the aridity of the place. I also noted that the window to Nadine's bedroom was open. Moving closer, snippets of conversation reached me intermittently, obscured in part by the whistling the heat produced in the foliage. I shot up the exterior stairs that led to the main floor. Opening the door, I entered the cool hallway and heard the purr of the air conditioner and that of Nadine's voice . . . the door to her bedroom was open and a heady odor of burnt oud drifted out. I hesitated to go any further . . . the fear of seeing them, the two of them, literally stopped me in my tracks . . . I listened carefully, trying to hear what was being said in the bedroom. I remained motionless on the threshold of their world, looking at that half-yawning door that I would only have to shove to catch them in the act . . . all I needed to do was stretch out my arm, by three feet, or even less . . . but my God those three feet seemed far!

Abdelkader, too, found the distance to be infinitely long when he stretched out his arm to push open the door of the

French Consulate in Damascus so he could propose raising an army of a thousand men and saving what remained to be saved of the Christians during that month of July in 1860. Infinitely long and infinitely short, as all the trajectories of his life seemed to converge toward that midafternoon when he went out onto his balcony and saw the Christian quarter burning, put to the torch and the sword, becoming a true charnel house under a cloud of brown smoke . . . infinitely short when his men informed him that the Russian Consulate was in flames, that the Dutch consul had been assassinated and that the rioters, the "rabble," as they said at the time, were scouring the city in search of the French consul to slit his throat. Infinitely short because he had to make the decision to go to the aid of the Christians in their need and despite the many vile abuses perpetrated on him by other Christians in other times, and which other Christians still continued to perpetrate, in Algeria . . . and on that balcony, on that scorching July day, over the whistling the heat produced in the trees of his garden, Abdelkader immediately knew that there were no parts within the whole that was unfolding by way of his existence and that a transcendental will gathered within it all the contrary wills that gave the impression of clashing with it . . . his own, that of the pasha, that of Louis-Napoléon, that of Bugeaud and of Lamoricière, those of the tribes of the east and those to the west . . . When he saw, from his balcony, his nephew's horrified face gasping for breath and come to let him know that the Christians were being murdered and their wives raped, he immediately understood which will it was that drove him to again take up his sword and go stand before the door of the French Consulate and stretch his arms wide so that in a few short hours his men stood tall before the dark rabble and his great dwelling was transformed into a replica of the

Château d'Amboise, within which thousands of Christians found refuge prior to being transferred to and protected behind the tall ramparts of Ahmed Pasha's citadel . . . and in a few days, after the Legion of Honor and the thanks of more or less every Christian in the world, the name Abdelkader was circulated around the luxurious cabinets of London and Paris in search of a consensus if not unanimity as to it being proclaimed that of the future governor of Syria concurrent with the establishment of Lebanon . . . When, in a few words, he revealed his disinterest and his withdrawal from political affairs: *That everyday life does not deceive you, that its vanities do not deceive you on the subject of God . . . My kingdom is not of this earth.*

Once I, in turn, pushed open the door, a violent shock passed through my chest as I saw them there, the two of them . . . Nadine, sitting cross-legged, passing her fingers through Mansour's hair . . . and the devastating effects of that shock spread to my stomach, like a heavy and nauseating echo, as I looked at Mansour's head resting on Nadine's thigh. When he saw me, Mansour didn't get up and Nadine didn't even bother to pull her hand away . . . as if they had foreseen my arrival and they had prepared themselves for it . . . she continued, without faltering, her monologue or her recitation or her prayer, while he peered up at me with a look that was both frightened and engrossed . . . like an animal fearing that his feed would be taken away or that his head would be cut off. Frozen there in the doorframe, I wordlessly watched the scene, which continued to unfold as if I wasn't even there. Nadine was caressing Mansour and reciting the poetry of Hafiz, Khayyám, Ibn 'Arabi, or the verses of a prayer to which only they understood the meaning and the words . . . in that position that left no doubt whatsoever as to their relationship . . . right in front of the friend that I quite suddenly no longer was.

Mansour, I can no longer exactly remember what forces were able to help me get back down the stairs after I fled your presence . . . what forces were there to support my legs, turned to ash by the shock, what forces were able to hold me up and carry me down to the bottom of the stairs where Ikram was waiting for me . . . and what forces urged me to speak to him. All the trajectories in this sky, Mansour, would have brought you to the center of this esplanade . . . Even if we had never left Damascus and even if you had never climbed atop that dune and if Ikram had never left his Pakistan, even if Nadine had written a thesis as dry as "The Logical Undecidability of Kantian Propositions," which would have inevitably led her to work in communications or advertising and would have allowed her to blossom in a hectic and exciting Paris where she would have made a life with someone exactly Stan's opposite . . . even if, Mansour, you and me, we would have both still ended up on this esplanade.

I was catching my breath at the bottom of the stairway when Ikram approached me and asked me if everything was all right, if I needed help. I looked at him for a long moment without being able to answer, I was still getting over my childish emotional outburst and saw something in his eyes that went beyond concern. Ikram was staring at me, scrutinizing my gestures and my attitude in search of the slightest discernable clue, the proof that would have allowed him to claim the five-hundred-riyal reward for denouncing something that was contrary to public morality . . . that is what I gathered from the look on his face and what frightened me. Our confrontation went on too long for it to end without consequences. Then I asked him if the two of them were often alone in that bedroom. Who's that? demanded Ikram, calmly and without really waiting for a response. The branches of the trees rustled in the heat and humidity of that accursed day and, before closing the gate of the villa, before returning to Mansour's Camaro, as I turned to see Ikram climbing the stairs, I wished with all of my heart that something might occur on those accursed stairs . . . that, even if it was the only time in the history of this accursed humanity, the path would lose itself in the infinite from which it was formed. But, just as the rustling of the trees didn't stop, Ikram continued to climb the stairs without losing himself in my imaginary world. Tears of childish rage ran down my cheeks as I closed the car door.

In tears, I asked myself why Providence had dropped us in this arid land when our destinies would have worked out much better in Dubai or Doha . . . like fish in the waters of that new Arab world, all aglitter and prosperous, filled with prostitutes and electronic music, where we would have found paradise in the bathroom of a nightclub or on the golden divans of a five star hotel as we enjoyed the sunset that cast its rays upon the sludgy and oily sea of the Persian Gulf which was little by little becoming the center of humanity . . . why did our luck run out two hundred and fifty miles from the heart of the galaxy, leaving us to toil away like slaves and paste whorish smiles onto our faces so that someone would offer us a glass or two of lousy whisky or lousy wine . . . and have us end up in this implausible story . . . In tears, I could once again see those that Mansour had let fall as he returned from atop his dune, toward which I was heading as fast as I could, for one more night . . . where I could cry at my leisure over this new world that was springing up as fast as it could over a sea made of sludge and petroleum and which, I had the feeling, the certitude, I would never see again . . . A terror-filled night awaited me atop the dune toward which I flew at full speed through the abrasive and absolute brilliance of the day that crashed down upon Mekkah Road . . . and in spite of all the sun that pasted itself across the windshield, which prevented me from seeing much of anything on that long road, I let loose all the horses of the Camaro . . . persuaded that nothing could happen to me because I had to be both source and witness to the passion of Mansour.

Gassouh! Gassouh!

8.

. . . HEAD THROWN BACK and eyes already closed, mouth open wide and neck extended, from which the silver cross hung and stirred and swung and waved to the thrusts of the animal he had become and that was trying to go even farther to push even deeper so as to enter into her as if it was a question of becoming her . . . the animal he had become grabbing hold with its entire body that of the one I desired with my entire soul and gluing its skin against hers and nuzzling its muzzle in a manner of speaking into her scented curls while keeping a fearful eye on the door and abruptly holding his hand or rather his paw across Nadine's mouth so as to disappear, the two of them, through moans and stifled cries . . . all of which I could hear in the wind that blew across that dune and in Mansour's voice which addressed, in short bursts, the cliffs of the Najd.

Gassouh! Gassouh! By the winds that blow once again and by the circles that are forming around you, by their rotation around the axis that will raise you up from among us, I swear to you, Mansour, that I knew nothing of the path to come! And I still don't know . . . if it leads from the center to the circumference or, just the opposite, if it means escaping the circumference to be reduced to the center. I was jealous of you, Mansour, but who wouldn't have been? It wasn't about her eyes, her skin, or her smell . . . You two were the center and the circumference brought into unity . . . what man among all of these men wouldn't have wanted to be the center and the circumference at the same time? You had known all too well the aimlessness of the single point and you know all of its misfortunes. Misfortune unto us, Mansour! Misfortune unto us! From atop your dune, Mansour, you continued to gather your words only to reveal them to me in unexpected ways, spontaneous, during what must have been your own sort of thinking . . . and your words, Mansour, as if reduced to their own essence, sounded astonishingly poetic. The few words that you uttered followed one behind the other as if to release something from within you . . . the image replaced the idea and the emotion became the message. Humanity's first word was poetic, and the last word will probably be *Gassouh*. Misfortune unto us, O God! Misfortune unto us!

Mansour read aloud, speaking the secrets revealed by the curvatures of the sand while I remained glued to Nadine's skin . . . imagining myself right next to it as Mansour's words took flight on the desert wind. Before the red patches of the sand, the pain she caused in me came in fits and starts. In one given moment, the desert would steal me away from myself . . . and then in the next moment, I would feel her burning beneath my skin. Burning from all that I continued to envision, as if I had been present in that bedroom where they must have loved each other until they disappeared, one and the other, among

the cries and eruptions of their bodies set free. And burning
by the side of the one who had been the source of all my suffering and who continued to provide me with the hot embers
upon which my desire was being consumed and upon which
my heart dreaded, worse than all of the bestiality that was being
revealed, that beaded in droplets off of the two lovers, worse
than the howls that must have floated up from their bodies . . .
worse than all of that, I feared to see Nadine lie down gently
on top of Mansour, who at that moment must have felt the
caress of her curls, felt the denseness of her hair flow across his
cheek as all of Nadine's warmth diffused from it . . . fearing
to see Nadine's lips slowly come to rest against Mansour's ear
to whisper into it something far more serious than the poetry
of Hafiz or Rumi or Khayyám, fearing to hear tender words,
words woven together like a chant, a canticle of canticles invit-
ing Mansour, begging him to come drink from her mouth the
finest of wines and become inebriated from all the love that
united them . . . in that bedchamber where Mansour had been
suddenly transfigured, passing suddenly from the animal into
Solomon himself, in that chamber of love where the smoke of
incense that enveloped the two lovers flowed across the floor, as
if prostrating itself before them, and where the books themselves
seemed to crawl and bow before what was going on above them
. . . before the miracle . . . Nadine and Mansour loved one
another to the point of disappearing one into the other, her into
him and him into her, to become one single and same being.
Venus climbed, alone, into a sky of bluish pink. Purplish-blue
glimmers were streaming across the rocky ramparts of the Najd
when Mansour turned to me. Where is all of it going? Brought
back to reality by his voice, I looked at the river of sand that
spread out around us and the raw beauty that it was setting free.

I turned back toward Mansour and noticed to what point he had been affected. As if he was returning from violent battles, his swollen and drooping eyelids holding up as best they could his sad and exhausted eyes . . . Where had he been? Where was he returning from? I had left him for a few short instants to transport myself into that bedroom and suffer the pains of love, a few short instants had been long enough for him to transport himself far beyond that point and far beyond all of the dunes . . . isolating himself right beside me and, at the same time, withdrawing into himself and opening himself up to the winds of the desert, like in some kind of act of contemplation or even meditation or both at the same time. Mansour had initiated an ascension, from state to state, which he was climbing in steps, in stations, so that the shock was not too violent, so that his mind or whatever was left of it or whatever it had become could adapt to what he was able to discover and know and see and feel . . . and to return from that voyage with something that seemed to me, once I had seen the glow of his eyes, to be astonishment or stupefaction . . . Fixed in place like a rock atop that dune, his eyes wide open and directed toward the cliffs, nothing whatsoever seemed to be stirring within him, not his body and not even his mind . . . his illness, the degeneration of his thinking matter, having surely provoked a reduction in the speed of his cerebral activity that would likely continue until it reached a complete standstill. Accordingly, time no longer held sway, he was becoming entirely enclosed in a kind of timeless transcendence. Through this, perhaps, he gained access to truths that were non-contingent and unbound to his history and his being. No longer being any more than a rock atop a dune made of sand, he no longer seemed to be inside himself. Where had he been? Where is all of it going? Mansour's voice reverberated dully, like an inaudible scream with no echo, aimed at the cliffs of the Najd.

Gassouh! Gassouh!

And then fearing even more than anything I had been able to imagine up to that point, more than the love that had been possible in spite of everything, seeing them once again from below the dune as if all three of us had been in that bedchamber that had suddenly become a sort of temple purified by oudwood incense where the large bed resembled a kind of sacrificial, or at least ritual, site and upon which they loved one another so tenderly that they had ended up disappearing . . . caressing one another with so much love so much kindness so much generosity so much gentleness and so much tenderness that they had ended up disappearing, one after the other, one with the other, one into the other, her into him and him into her . . . loving one another so strongly that they became one with the One. And me, from a corner of the bedroom, seeing them consume one another, right before my eyes, like two butterflies in the flames . . . from atop this dune, I feared that there had been between them something much stronger than love . . . dreading that, in Mansour's mind, loving Nadine amounted to loving the Divine Creator, amounted to loving Creation in its entirety. Above the sands, his gaze directed toward the plateau that rose up before us, Mansour once more expressed something that must have been the representation, the result, or the condensed version of a state he had reached . . . All worship is but worship of the essence of the Creator. All love is but love of Him.

I knew nothing of the path, Mansour . . . and I swear to you, Mansour, that I would have done things in the opposite direction if the structure of time had allowed me. How is it possible for us to do the opposite of what we want to do? How was it possible for me to wind up there, how was it possible for me to send you to the center of this esplanade . . . to send you to prostrate yourself before this crowd of unbelievers, to bow your head, to stretch out your neck for the blade of the traitors! Even though I am first among them, the first traitor, the one who would deserve the spit and the mud. Do you remember, Mansour, when we were in Damascus and you told me the story of your illustrious ancestor? When you described for me the eyes that the Duke of Aumale must have had when he was given Emir Abdelkader's weapons and when he promised him exile to Saint Jean d'Acre or somewhere else in the East . . . Well, I most certainly must have had those same eyes when, from atop your dune, you shared with me the words that had come from Nadine's lips . . . You said that the eyes of the French duke had looked condescendingly over all that made up the village of Ghazaouet and that they had abruptly widened when Abdelkader presented himself before him, like a pale star climbing the night sky. The duke's bright eyes expressed all of his admiration and his fascination and then, when Abdelkader handed him his saber, reminding him of Lamoricière's promise, darting and shifty, they no longer expressed anything but envy and shame . . . the shame of an entire nation. You said he was envious in the face of Abdelkader's words and eyes, convinced that such a man would never go back on his oath, you said he was envious of the power of the promise and ashamed to know himself incapable of keeping his own. I have no kingdom, Mansour, but my eyes, from atop that dune, must have certainly expressed just as much envy and shame when they met your own . . . envious and jealous of all the love that had been given to you and ashamed to want to take it away from you . . . But I know that your eyes knew all of that when they met my own. You are the only one to have tasted of Nadine's lips, you are the only one to have known the marvel of love, you are the only one to have known the raptures of faith . . . out of all of us, you are the one true believer. We are the traitors, who have renounced much more than our faith.

And then reappearing, the two of them, before my eyes and on the slope of sand that gave me the impression it wanted to swallow me up. I saw that bedchamber once more, where Nadine, sitting cross-legged on that large unmade bed, still trying to catch her breath and still sweating, held Mansour's head . . . which he had, just then, completely exhausted, rested on one of her thighs as if he had set it there after it had been severed by the violence of ecstasy . . . she gathered him up in her hands like Leila might have done with the fallen of Love, or like Rabiʿah, the first female saint of Islam, who rested her body and head against the earth during prayer. From one of the corners of that chamber of love, I read in the curls of smoke given form by the incense all that was signified by the position of the two lovers . . . And I heard, with tears in my eyes, Nadine's voice. *From Your love, I am given life. From my love, you are given Yours.*

Gassouh! Gassouh!

I fell from atop your dune and I tumbled down the never-ending slope. I fell suddenly as a result of moving in your direction or maybe from trying to get up from that uncomfortable, unbearable position, from that oh-so fragile balance upon the line that divided the two sides of your dune . . . worn out, crushed by everything that I had just seen or imagined, heard or fantasized, I had wanted to get up to leave or maybe I had wanted to charge at you . . . Whatever the case, I stumbled and fell from the top of your dune and rolled like a stone, no more and no less than a stone, which tumbled down that never-ending slope to end up like a man in the sea, and I sank into the sands of that long dried-up river, terrified and fearing that it might carry me off into the emptiness of the desert. In that mineral void where I felt as if I was drowning, I tried to save myself by attempting to climb back up, to travel in reverse up that bank from which I had plummeted like a falling stone. I was laboriously climbing the dune where you, Mansour, still rested, sitting lightly and, while I continued to toil away, to sink into the goldenness of the sand, to struggle for breath as I tried to attract your attention, you turned your gaze on me like you were holding out a hand, at once open and closed . . . And whatever the case, I remained full of fear and full of rage and full of images that overlaid themselves upon the distribution, the undulation, the *sinuation* of the sands and the rocks that sprawled the length of a red and ochre immensity alongside a sun descending and diffusing its gentle rays that spread wide and setting in long sweeps across the majestic cliffs of the Najd which also stretched out, rolled out reproduced in waves forming gigantic dizzying ridges escarpments that threaded and dashed their way across that vast expanse of sand beyond which towered yet more majestic cliffs from another plateau like two banks two shorelines of the great river that had noisily flowed centuries and centuries earlier and which had since become nothing more than a graceful and undulating succession of dunes, curved and dry and flowing toward the infinite that unfurled itself everywhere my eyes could turn . . . Your hand, right then, caught my own . . . and your eyes, Mansour, grabbed on to mine. A battle's conclusion. Your eyes were nothing less than the manifestation, at least to my senses drowned in the waves and the eddies of sand, of a power that rises up past the heavens . . . Your eyes were at once the supreme image and the veil in front of the supreme image.

In that waning daylight, I could see nothing but the light of your eyes. Your eyes of love. I surfaced from the waves and drew up alongside you . . . I put my footsteps in yours so as to once again find my way to the city where the two of us had washed up.

9.

BY THE SUN THAT SETS and by its descending rays. By the flash of the light before the morbid darkness. By the sun that rises and the truth it reveals. By the flash of light behind the perishing darkness. An idiotic smile . . . there, perhaps that is the only thing that history will remember of President François Hollande. Mansour and I have been too hard and too unfair as far as he is concerned, too mocking, even, when it surely must have been his readings of history and his left-wing revolutionary thinking that had shaped his convictions in such a way that he came to the aid of the people of Syria . . . not only the devotion to defending human rights but also some deeper conviction, more concrete, like an old debt that France needed to repay and that he, friendly François of the Français, had resolved to take on himself, personally . . . perhaps, even more than to eliminate the dishonor, it was to erase the breaking of a sworn oath, that of Lamoricière or that of the Duke of Aumale, it was for something more integral in the French identity that this friendly little fellow had substantially raised himself up to become the savior of the Syrian people . . . for a fitting bit of poetic justice. A return to grace. In the same way that Abdelkader had saved thousands of Christians from certain massacre, François felt duty-bound to save thousands of Syrians from massacres to come. Poetic justice toward history. That was definitely it. How had we been so stupid and so mocking when we knew perfectly well that in politics, decisions are made in accordance with three or four different priorities, in terms of convenient truth and not absolute . . . stupid and mocking even as we wandered through labyrinths of logic that pushed us to believe he only adopted that position to do business with the Saudis or to protect Israel or to ensure himself a second term in office, a lightning-quick war like in Mali that would guarantee him unquestionable popularity and a re-election that was just as unquestioned . . . stupidly mocking.

But you hadn't yet become what you were destined to become. By the sun that was setting and by the cold that was returning, I was emerging from the waves of sand and I put my footsteps in yours so as to once again climb that dune where I had sought out the point from which it seemed to me that you could see the truth stripped bare . . . but had I truly found it, that point? Because around me, there was nothing but desert. Emptiness as far as the eye could see. And I told myself that perhaps this was what you had been seeking. Not the infinite beauty of that empty infinite, but the emptiness itself. And to take refuge within it. Mansour, you were falling from atop that dune into an unfathomable void without my even being able to notice it happening. And there you resided in the company of the truth stripped bare. And when you returned to me, in that waning daylight, I could see nothing but the light of your eyes

. . . and in your eyes, Mansour, I could see nothing but your love. As I sank into the sands, you came down from atop your dune with the elegance of a tightrope walker and the grace of an angel. You hadn't yet become what you were destined to become. How can one grasp the center and the circumference at the same time? How is it possible, in a single motion, to reduce oneself to be the center while expanding oneself to be the circumference? And that is definitely what you succeeded in doing atop your dune, curling yourself up so as to unfurl like a shockwave across the infinite expanse of sand . . . *Gassouh!* cry the fools instead of prostrating themselves around you and begging a few atoms of your knowledge. Even just a single atom of your knowledge.

Or perhaps François' smile conveyed a profound lack of understanding of things and in particular of the world, which had to continue spinning too quickly, so to speak, and for which he had neither the strength nor the intelligence to slow it down, to attempt to understand it more subtly, more plainly, more justly . . . much like Mansour and I, François wouldn't understand anything at all about anything at all and he was all too conscious of his own inability to have a vision, even if it was only a simple glimmer of a vision . . . knowing only that he had to get over it without thinking too much about his minister's decisions or those of his advisers and that he had nothing more than that idiotic smile to offer to the world . . . nothing more than that idiotic smile, like an avowal of impotence, polite and full of excuses, in the face of the world and his advisers, young thirty-somethings or barely forty, in a hurry to move at the same rhythm as this new world and in a hurry to be done with the old political system that he incarnated in spite of the hair dyeing and the clever jokes that livened up his speeches and the occasional peals of laughter that he still managed to elicit . . . so that idiotic smile he offered up to young forty-somethings like Mansour and me, thinking that perhaps he was dealing with two advisers from Syria or Lebanon or Jordan when in fact we were, just like him, in the middle of sinking into total incomprehension with regard to anything that went on around us . . . just as lost as him, all we had left was mockery when it came to believing that we still understood something about this disturbing world in which we no longer had any role to play and in which we had become nothing more than extras, blended into the background of an artificially sparkling set . . . just like the Caliph al-Muqtadir, without power and without authority, we imagined François skulking around inside the walls of the Élysée without even being permitted to attend crucial meetings . . . Just as impotent as al-Muqtadir, in other times and other places, François would have recovered amid the sensuous tenderness of a harem.

Abdelkader covered his head with a white veil when he hoped, he too, to reduce himself to the center of things by expanding himself to their circumference. Sitting in a corner of one of the rooms of that immense Château d'Amboise where the French had contained him, so to speak, he rested across his knees the little lap-top writing desk, upon which he unrolled some paper to keep up his correspondence and the hope that someone would one day heed his call . . . and in spite of the comings and goings and the commotion of his entire *smala*, he managed to find the words and to hear the Loire flowing outside his window . . . *Émile Ollivier, your emissary, came to see me and informed me that the French, in one single agreement, have abolished the royalty and decreed that their country will henceforth be a Republic. I rejoiced in this news as I have read in books that this form of government has as its goal the eradication of injustices, and aims to prevent the strong from doing violence upon the weak. You are generous men and you desire the best for all and your actions are dictated by the spirit of justice.* It was in words like these, although at the time I wasn't quite aware of it, that the voice of Abdelkader lived on in the mind of François Hollande and pushed him to act in Syria . . . or to allow himself to be pushed to act . . . because how else could it have come to pass? We had foolishly forgotten to consider the spirit of justice that had always made up the backbone of his thinking, Mansour and I . . . the spirit of justice, from the time he began as a young student at boarding school right up until he left the École Nationale d'Administration to make his rise through the Parti Socialiste and become embodied by a constantly benevolent smile. Why had we been so awful and so full of mockery?

By mistake . . . *Gassouh!* What a mistake, what a giant mistake! My God, we are so often mistaken . . . it takes so little, the smallest argument, as insignificant as it may be, only slightly erroneous but sufficient to divert our trajectory away from the truth . . . for all of the rationality of the world, the most rigorous, to not be able to bring us back to the truth. Like after that blade, Mansour, after its passage, all my tears, no matter how full of pain, will not be able to bring you back to life. *Gassouh! Gassouh!* cry in one voice the fools who have not considered for one instant the possibility that there has been a mistake. The heat rises, suffocating. Is that all you feel? The rage and the hatred, beneath this uncompromising sun, make the entire crowd sweat like livestock . . . But are they all you feel? *Gassouh!* Like it is the only word that is true to life among this congregation of Muslims. Only a few yards now separate you from the center of the esplanade . . . scarcely a few yards. That's the sole truth of this moment. But is that the sole truth you know?

By the sun that sets and by its declining rays. By the flash of the light before the morbid darkness. By the sun that rises and the truth it reveals. By the flash of light behind the perishing darkness. One hand holding the decorative trim of his white burnoose, and the other, a black string of prayer beads. This was how Abdelkader looked during the last thirty years of his life, and this was the image that would remain of him in the minds of those who had known him and who would remember the story before the memory of this great man disappeared. It was in the company of this idea that I sat down and tried to remain, atop Mansour's dune, thinking that there was not a more legitimate place for me to be prior to making my way to the trial. Abdelkader remained hours at a time on the cold tiling of the Umayyad Mosque as if he was sitting at the summit of a dune from which he could contemplate the vast country to which he had in a manner of speaking given birth and perhaps even read in the variations of the wind or in the declinations of the sun or in the serpentine meanderings of the sands all of the future that was traced therein . . . but he remained on that cold tiling in one of the corners of the great Umayyad Mosque to contemplate the millions of intersections of the interlacing that the gigantic friezes revealed to his eyes and in which he could read all of the past and all of the future that was traced therein . . . *Having reached that state of euphoria, of effacement, of non-being, I reached that which is now, in truth, neither place nor beyond . . . The vertical and the horizontal annihilated one another. The colors returned to pure primordial whiteness. All ambition, all relations abolished, the original state is reestablished. The voyage has reached its end and that which is other than Him has ceased to exist.* And when his heart became capable of welcoming all representation, when it became a vast pasture for galloping gazelles, a shelter for isolated souls and a monastery for penitent monks . . . when his heart became the Mecca of pilgrims and the tables of the Torah and a volume of the Qur'an . . . when his heart became vast enough to contain the love of humanity in its entirety, there was no longer room for anything but the love of God.

Ikram, for five hundred riyals, had sent us all before the morality case judge of the Governorate of Riyadh for the protection of morals and religion or, maybe, the committee for the promotion of virtue and the prevention of vice, which is to say to a dark chamber, entirely without prestige, where dozens of defendants were squeezed in before a simple desk from behind which Judge Abou Daoud al-Qassimi listened to the lawyers, briefly cast an eye over the dossiers or law books, raised his head, adjusted his white *shemagh* and pronounced his judgment . . . in an expeditious manner, we feared, from the other side of the desk . . . Mansour, Nadine, veiled from head to toe, Stan, redder than a beet, and the consul of Australia, flanked by two bodyguards . . . and me a bit farther away and Ikram even farther away . . . After having stated the alleged facts of the case, Abou Daoud, playing the part of tribunal president in this sad place that played the part of a courtroom, asked Ikram to come forward to him and make known what it was he had to make known. In a structureless Arabic, made up simply of verbs and subjects and religious clichés, Ikram found enough words to make it understood that Nadine and Mansour had engaged in an adulterous relationship . . . this broken Arabic would amply suffice when it came to earning the two lovers a hundred lashes of the whip and him pocketing five hundred riyals. The president then asked Nadine to introduce herself. Which she did, briefly, with a noble look and terribly sad eyes . . . I am Nadine Nasr, an Australian originally from Lebanon,

Christian, thirty-nine years old. Married to Stan Vaughan, present here today? asked Abou Daoud. Nadine then turned her head toward Mansour, who was standing hardly six feet away from her, encountered gleaming eyes, and replied: Yes, Mister President! He then turned in Mansour's direction and asked him to present himself. Mansour broke away from Nadine's eyes, looked at me and then looked at the lawyer who had been appointed to him, then the spectators, and stated his identity . . . I am Mansour al-Jazaïri . . . Mansour bin Soltane bin Hassan bin Mohamed bin Abdelkader . . . I am of him . . . I am him. A muted buzz rose from the audience signaling a sort of indignation that the president pacified by holding up an open hand and asking: You are Him? or not really asking but simply exclaiming: You are Him! and keeping his open hand held out to the twenty or so people who happened to be there and who were witnessing what I then took as some kind of disastrous absolute, a suicide. The Australian consul rapidly approached the judge and secretly spoke with him, in a hushed voice, for several long minutes, in the silence of that sad hearing room. Mansour looked at me with a smile that was at once strange and benevolent. The judge stood up and explained that Nadine had fallen prey to the influence of a heretic and that consequently he declared her not answerable and signed her banishment from the kingdom . . . as for Mansour, he ordered him to be placed in detention pending his trial for heresy which would take place in the near future. Two guards fell upon Mansour to remove him while he continued to cling, with his eyes, to Nadine's. In a few seconds, all had disappeared. I remained, alone, in the middle of that dim room where the melee had resumed and where the judgments came one after another in a sustained pace. I stayed on a few hours in that dark and lowly chamber, stunned, unable to leave. When I was finally able, Abou Daoud's gaze caught my own and I understood that there was no hope.

The red Camaro had me across Riyadh in a flash and I fell into my bed just as quickly. That night, in my dreams, I saw myself lying down in that vast desert expanse that I visited almost every day. Stretched out, alone and naked and hearing the sound of hooves approaching me . . . alone and naked, I looked at the blue sky and asked myself how the hooves could make such a noise on the sand . . . alone and naked, I turned my head toward the sound of the hooves and I saw a horse mounted by a strange costumed rider . . . alone and naked and dumbfounded by the sound of hooves and the garb of that strange rider in that place and in that heat. Coming within a few yards of me, the strange rider, who turned out to be François Hollande, dismounted his steed, which turned out to be an ass. The heat of the desert clouded my vision to the point that I saw my two visitors undulating . . . I wanted to get up and take flight but it was in vain. I remained there, frozen, as if made of stone, watching the ass advance in its disturbing undulation. Powerless, I watched it advance and stop above me. Its shadow protected me from the sun and I could feel an unexpected coolness travel across my whole body . . . it made me shiver. François too had advanced to stand next to me. And I didn't stop shivering when the ass began nibbling something and I didn't stop shivering even as I asked myself what he could possibly be grazing on in this expanse of sand . . . and it was without any pain that I understood that the ass was calmly eating my head while François smiled at me peacefully, amiably, full of benevolence and love. When I awoke, François Hollande's idiotic smile haunted me all the way to Kingdom Hospital from which, in a manner of speaking, I kidnapped Maarafi from his consultations to rush over to see the qadi Abou Daoud al-Qas-simi and to convince him, to beg him, to cancel this trial where Mansour wasn't running the risk of a few lashes of the whip and expulsion from the country but well and truly his head. Despite being refused entry, I made my way into the judge's office, into that hole, looked with wariness at the thousands of pages spread out on the table and wondered how he managed to find anything among them or to understand anything about the cases he handled and if he was going to know who it was we meant to speak to him about and for whom we were about to ask for mercy . . . but he knew perfectly well, he grasped it with a first look, without even leaving us the time to present ourselves, he understood that we had come for my friend and he asked us to sit down around that table where the thousands of sheets had accumulated, piled and heaped to form irregular stacks and among which, on one of them, Mansour's name was most certainly inscribed. Looking me straight in the eye, he told me that the phrase had been uttered, that the words had been let out and that we couldn't go backwards . . . Looking him straight in the eye, I asked him where those words were now, in what world they continued to resonate, in what place had they ended up . . . Looking me straight in the eye, Abou Daoud replied that God had heard them and that he expected just reparations . . . lowering my eyes, I already regretted not being able to better express my rage and my incomprehension when it came to the continuously variable weight of speech when I remembered, neither daring to mention it nor make reference to it, the word of Abdelkader and that of the Duke of Aumale, Faisal's speech and that of François . . . and yet I would have liked to speak about the unspoken words of the great Arab-Muslim civilization, to speak about all those words that no one heard anymore, I would have even liked to speak about all the words that circulated without end and without the slightest weight in mall talk on advertising posters in newspapers on radio waves and on television screens and, worse still, about all those words spewing across page after page of social media, without even the life expectancy of a gnat, not even that of a mayfly, and no more distinguished than a grain of sand . . . yes, about all those words flitting and darting about like billions upon billions of grains of sand, without weight and without consequence, falling like common refuse onto the vast avenues of Riyadh . . . or, for that matter, not falling at all, carried off into a void adjacent to the void of the desert . . . I lowered my eyes and felt deceived for having thought that a spoken word had no more weight than a grain of sand that flew about above a dune . . . As I lowered my eyes, I got the impression that I was closing them in the grayish dimness of that office that looked more like a tomb . . . From the implausible jumble of papers, Abou Daoud's hand, without hesitating or trembling, pulled out a single one. He held it out to me. Mansour's name was written on it and, just below it, there were two short phrases. *I am of him. I am him.* Then there were Maarafi's attempts to take control of the situation and Judge Abou Daoud al-Qassimi's tears, there was an exchange of the words of God and an interminable wait . . . but it was all in vain. I took Maarafi back and returned to the dune, the site of my earlier collapse, and there I spent several long sleepless nights.

By the day that endlessly sets and by that which endlessly rises, I swear that I remained entire nights atop your dune. And even that my days had become somber nights. Those hundred hours separating your two trials spent praying to God and his Creation for your acquittal . . . imploring his forgiveness and begging his mercy. Without drinking and without eating and without sleeping among the winds that swept across the sands of your dune, I remained to beg for your forgiveness and your mercy . . . and I am here this morning, right near you, and I again beg all that you can grant me as far as forgiveness and love . . . and I am here this morning and my desire to leave with you is killing me. Take me with you, Mansour, I won't be any heavier than a grain of sand . . . I have so little strength left, Mansour, that you'll have no difficulty lifting me up from down here.

10.

RIYADH IS A DUSTY WHITE GRID where, once you've gotten underway, because of the gradual narrowing of the avenues and the streets, you always end up landing in the heart of the city. That heart, Old Deerah, is a cluster of dilapidated buildings crammed with thousands of laborers, small-timers, heavy lifters, shopkeepers, street vendors, and odd-job handymen, buildings which line what used to be the bed of a river and its tributaries, al-Batha. Frenzied circulation, night and day, provides the beat of this heart . . . but it beats no longer since they brought you out of your cell and you began your bowed march toward the center of the esplanade. What made up the blood of al-Batha has solidified, coagulated around a mat you're walking toward and from which you are no longer very far. The crowd is only holding its breath so that it can better erupt with joy when your head falls. A silence that you notice over the sound of your chains and the noise of the winds trapped in Al Safat Square. Riyadh, a grid in motion, a dust trap in which I have become stuck, one that has sucked me all the way in to its heart . . . all the way to here. Near you.

By way of the same dusty grid, as I arrived at the Deerah courthouse, I was astonished to find Maarafi in the gradually filling waiting room. I have something important to tell you! he announced, leading me away from the court's employees, who always managed, he added, to leave an ear lying around where it wasn't wanted. It is possible to interpret the tests in a completely different way . . . Your friend may not be a fool after all! There is something we can attempt to save him. I looked at him silently for a long while without understanding, as my vision blurred and everything grew dark around Maarafi's smiling face until it all dissolved into a disturbing blackness, a symptom of the malaise that nearly made me faint . . . All I could see was an intense blackness out of which little sparks shot and then disappeared, leaving behind them ephemeral traces of their trajectories . . . An indescribable anguish engulfed me . . . That's worse . . . I told him, without conviction and struggling to collect my wits. Not at all! Don't forget, Abou Daoud is a sensitive man, and we can make him believe that your friend has been the victim of a scientific error, an error of modernity, of machines programmed by unbelievers . . . or that the tests weren't adapted to our way of thinking, that of our culture and our beliefs . . . Mansour's lawyer had just joined us at that moment, which allowed me to avoid going any further into the discussion by leaving the two of them to go to the restroom. I shut myself in there to get stoned in the hope that it would help me get through this day that I sensed was going to be terrible. I could hear the grating sound of the scraper that the janitor was energetically using on the floor. The smoke built up in my stall where I sat thinking of how badly it must have reeked, that characteristic stench of burnt leaves and damp wood . . . As I watched the smoke seep under the door, I threw the joint into the toilet bowl and pulled the chain to flush it. On my way out, the janitor stared at me defiantly, letting me know that he had understood what was going on . . . Surprisingly sure of myself, I returned his stare, without knowing what sign had convinced me he wouldn't say anything about it. And without knowing why, I smiled at him and left. I found Maarafi and the little ulama appointed to defend Mansour's rights debating the correct strategy to adopt in hopes of avoiding the worst . . . but I didn't have the brain-power or the clear-sightedness or the strength to resolve the quandaries which they seemed to be confronting. Roughly, it was a question of either passing Mansour off as being mentally ill in hopes of arousing the pity of the court, or of painting him as a victim, but one who had been in possession of all his facul-ties at the moment in question . . . and once more, their faces slipped back behind that darkness where the sparks traced their ephemeral and convergent trajectories. A bad sign, I started to tell myself before I was interrupted by Maarafi, who wanted my opinion to help settle the question . . . but I didn't know what to reply. I was worried to see those trajectories converge toward a small, dark disk suspended in the middle of my field of vision. I left them once again to go splash some water on my face and recover a bit of lucidity. When I returned, Maarafi again asked my opinion, which I did not have time to give because by this point, Mansour's lawyer seemed more set on the strategy to adopt. He brushed aside any idea of a quandary because, according to him, the accused only needed to reiterate a pro-fession of Muslim faith and make an act of contrition before everyone present, after which he would be acquitted. However, Maarafi still continued to elaborate his own idea without me really grasping its utility. He was all twisted up in knots, feeling perhaps that he was responsible for all of this . . . But I didn't have time to find out any more, either. An employee of the tribunal opened the door to the hearing room and invited us to enter.

I was surprised to find a lot of people inside . . . Thinking at first that they were defendants waiting for their turn, I soon understood that it was actually a public invited especially for the trial. Behind the reading desk where Abou Daoud al-Qassimi delivered his judgments, they had set up mats and Bedouin cushions in red and black, embroidered with gold thread. In front of the reading desk, they had also installed a kind of bar that the witnesses and the accused could lean against . . . they had wanted, evidently, to make a spectacle out of it. Rows of chairs, here and there, filled the hearing room, which was still entirely without prestige. The staff member showed us to our places while Abou Daoud sat silently behind his desk, seeming to wait for the VIPs who would park their asses on the gold-embroidered mats. Two other judges entered, took their positions next to Abou Daoud, and they waited as well. The ambiance of a long-gone era gradually came over the place without us noticing the details. It was as if we had been propelled back a thousand years into the past, into the days of the Abbasid Caliphs, the days of al-Muktafi or al-Muqtadir, the days when the first enemy of a Muslim was another Muslim, the days of the Qarmatians and the Zanj, in the days of denominational uproar and bloody revolts where despite everything they attempted to preserve the wealth of Arab knowledge of that stunningly contradictory tenth century . . . That tenth century where the houses of wisdom abutted the Caliphate jails and where every learned man could, from the silence of his contemplation, hear the cries of the tortured. Each learned man, to gain entrance into those houses of wisdom, simply had to hold out his arm and push open the door, above which it was no longer necessary to write that no one ignorant of geometry was to enter, because the ornamentation was so eminently geometrical . . . These same ornamentations were replicated in friezes, mosaics, and tiling in all the great mosques of the empire, if not to forewarn, then to remind every Muslim that he was entering a place of prayer, of worship and reflection . . . while only a few yards away, the blood of the tortured soiled the marble of the dynasty's esplanades . . . That completely incomprehensible tenth century. Eventually, a delegation clearly made up of members of the royal family and several ulamas, after having greeted the three judges, hastened to take their places on the raised mats and to give the go-ahead for the heresy trial. Then Mansour was led in. Head shorn and wearing a long white tunic. Shorn like an animal. He was seated in the front row, beside the stranger who had been appointed as his defense, and Abou Daoud launched into a long introduction during which he reminded everyone of the principal tenets of the religion, the pillars that every Muslim was bound to protect, body and soul . . . and then, perhaps because of the lack of sleep or because of what I had recently smoked, I switched off, so to speak, and could from then on grasp only discontinuous sequences of reality and of the time that shaped it . . . Mansour's shaved head, Maarafi's outbursts, Abou Daoud's moving lips, the drab walls of the tribunal chamber, Maarafi's inopportune whispering . . . Time had lost all of the continuity that composed it and I no longer had the mental acuity or the energy to put it back together. I drifted, from one moment to another, from one image to another and from one sentence to another without there being the slightest link or connection or meaning . . . and I only vaguely understood the point of the trial . . . or rather, I understood that there really wasn't one, that Abou Daoud wanted to make Mansour confess, wanted him to admit his crime so that he would be saved, or so that his soul would be, so that he might escape the anathema and perish instead by way of the purifying saber . . . and I felt Maarafi leap up at every contradiction and I felt myself drift away until the moment Abou Daoud called me forward to the bar.

Even the purest of geometries break down, sometimes, into crude scribbles.

How long it seemed to take and how endless a path for me to arrive in front of the three judges who interrogated me as witness to the life of Mansour. That suspended time during which I'm not sure by what miracle I had remembered the first trial of Mansur al-Hallaj, that time just full enough of gaps for me to remember the pretext that the Vizier Nasr had found so as to avoid the death of someone with whom he was close . . . and on that little stage, as I faced all of those who awaited my responses, when I opened my mouth to speak, the word *jahil*, ignorant, slipped out like a sigh of relief . . . And so I described Mansour's life as that of an ignorant man who passed his days in the mall spending his money indiscriminately, which was his only passion, the only meaning in his life . . . I expressed loud and clear that Mansour had neither the time nor the desire to concern himself with religion, that he knew nothing about anything, and specified, along the way, that he drank whenever the opportunity presented itself and that he never prayed . . . thinking, naively but sincerely, that if the use of *jahil* had worked in the days of al-Hallaj, then it was because it must appear in the legal texts, in black and white, irrefutable . . . I continued, specifying that Mansour had never received a proper Muslim education, that he had been schooled by the French in Damascus, and I overstated the attributes of a life of debauchery by revealing that he sometimes visited the whores in Bahrain and that he was well known at the French Embassy because of his rather undiplomatic drinking sprees. Can we judge an ignorant man? I asked. One of the members of the royal family stood up at that moment, went over to Abou Daoud and whispered something to him. The president then thanked me for the clarification I had just provided to the court and summoned Mansour to the bar to verify, he said, the extent of his religious knowledge. I saw Mansour's shaved head and I heard his voice state his faith in Islam and recite the Surah of Light to the courtroom, silent and astonished. I saw Mansour's head and everything plunged back into the darkness, everything fell apart, returned to its starting point.

A scribble teeming with lines, verging on total blackness.

You have arrived at the center, Mansour. You're there! Your executioner is a giant who holds you in place by the strength of his arm alone. He's wearing a long white tunic covered by a black cape embroidered with gold, he has a *shemagh* rolled around his head and he holds a long saber with his other arm. But you don't see any of it. You're standing up straight, your head lowered and your eyes riveted on the unrolled mat that is to collect your parts . . . Just like yesterday, when you stood up straight, head lowered and eyes riveted to the floor of that sad tribunal chamber where, across from you, the judges likely hoped to meet your gaze so they could see what kind of eyes you were made of. As if you were at prayer, you offered them nothing but your words . . . and those were as clear as your eyes. The wind picks up around us more and more and the billions upon billions of grains of dust multiply themselves in order to become the visible atoms of this reality. Your executioner releases you from your chains and yet you appear more enchained than before . . . Your executioner, with an abrupt gesture, rids you of the veil that covers your head and you suddenly seem naked . . . naked and at prayer, eyes riveted to the mat that is to collect your parts and, just like yesterday, you stand as straight as the line of a destiny. Just like yesterday, when you stood up straight, head lowered and eyes riveted to the floor of that sad tribunal chamber where, across from you, the judges likely hoped they could see what kind of eyes you were made of but you offered them nothing more than your words . . . I found myself to be sand among the sands . . . Violent pains came to slow my frantic flight and to retrace the trajectory my destiny was following. Those violent pains were the manifestation of a miracle. And I found myself to be sand among the sands . . . I sank into incomprehension of everything that surrounded me. I questioned myself about the simplest things without grasping even the least bit of their meaning. And yet I possessed, as a legacy, all the wisdom of our ancestors and all the words of those who had shaped our civilization. But I had never known how to read them . . . and I found myself to be sand among the sands. Until Nadine appeared to me. Like a miracle. Her fingertips guided me along the lines of the open books and her lips opened my heart . . . and I was remade, reassembled, from among the sands, by His will alone!

Or perhaps you said nothing, Mansour. Mute and stunned, as would be an animal that has strayed into a courthouse. Or perhaps you only managed to pronounce a few words. Nearly inaudible. Her . . . Him . . . Me . . . His will . . . And you again recited the Surah of Light before the distraught eyes of Abou Daoud.

Be quiet! one of the two judges seated beside Abou Daoud had cried. How can you associate this adultery with the will of the Almighty? It all seemed so unreal to me, Mansour, when the people present in that room began to shout as well and when the guards had to come in to reestablish order. One of the other two judges had begun to recite verses from the Qur'an and to explain them, in order to reestablish serenity and calm, he clarified, so as to carry on with the trial under the best possible conditions. It all seemed so unreal to me, Mansour, I didn't understand anything about anything. And I also didn't under-stand what you had just revealed to us . . . Her fingertips guided me along the lines of the open books and her lips opened my heart . . . and I was remade, reassembled, from among the sands, by His will alone! Images superimposed themselves on the yellowed walls of that hearing room, which reeked of the Old Kingdom, while the judge continued his recitation and while I pictured you atop your dune, following the thread of your thoughts, continuously, until an accident took place, until an unexpected leap revealed something else to you, something out of the ordinary, a moment outside of time that was maybe equivalent to the one experienced by Poincaré in Coutances, when he was preparing to leave on a walk with his friends to take a break and forget about his mathematical work, which wasn't progressing, when he was about to climb up into the bus that was to take them, he and his group of friends, gathered together in a vacation-like ambiance, festive and happy and carefree, right up until the moment he took that famous step which was to reveal to him, in a manner that was as unexpected as it was powerful, the connection between Fuchsian functions and non-Euclidian geometry. That moment of madness and rapture was perhaps the same as the one that removed you from the world, from atop that dune, as you stared out onto the cliffs of the Najd. Or perhaps it was God, did he reveal Himself atop that dune, by way of a voice or an image, allowing you to clearly understand His will? . . . and it wasn't that tale of adultery, vulgarly associated with the name of God, that provoked the indignation and the condemnation of that old hearing room but rather the fact that God had revealed himself before you that they found unbearable . . . much as with Emir Abdelkader, who they reproached not for his surrender so much as for the way he explained it: *When God enjoined me to stand up, I stood up. I went the way of the gun to the far limits of my means and my possibilities. But when He ordered me to cease, I stopped . . . and I gave myself up* . . . How had God ordered, spoken, to he who was after all, in the eyes of his fellows, no more than a nomad like they were, an Arab like they were? And how did God reveal himself to you and through you, the ignorant man, the Arab?

It all seemed so unreal to me and I no longer understand much of anything at all about how the trial unfolded. A headache progressively set in and a strange sound resonated in my brain . . . and I could feel it vibrate, actually, as if echoing the strange *ziiiiiin* or *zooooon* sound, that continuous and metallic noise that grew louder as the judge continued his lengthy lecture, which seemed like a torture he wished to inflict upon us before returning the floor to the accused. Abou Daoud then asked Mansour to clarify the phrases he had spoken at the initial trial, which the judge seemed reluctant to bring up but did so all the same, his lips moving reticently and to the indignation of all of the believers who begged forgiveness of God for having heard such words. Mansour remained silent, or at least it seemed so to me, for a good long moment. Maarafi whispered something into my ear once again but I didn't understand it . . . he insisted a second time then turned to the lawyer. I sensed something terrible was happening without it frightening me any more than you would expect and everything, without my truly grasping the meaning, seemed to unfold along a straight-line trajectory, as straight as the line of a destiny. Although this representation allows you to see my appearance, it cannot offer you our supreme image. For behind what you see lies a veiled personality. That, all in all, is what I had expressed through the sentences you reproach me for, Mansour had finally admitted, after that long silence. And if, at that moment, I still understood anything, it seemed to me that he had specified having heard that one day when he had felt completely abandoned by God. That terrifying image had left him on the ground, in the street, in front of a mall and in front of dozens of people whom he already saw as dead . . . Dead who wouldn't even make up the humus of our earth. Old, dry bones that would end up as sand . . . on that earth where God's desertion seemed absolute to me. And it seemed imperative that I affirm God at a time when he had disappeared from the world . . . by saying "I am Him." New protests rang out in the chamber and Abou Daoud interrupted Mansour by asking him, now that he had admitted and detailed the facts, to repent by praying for the mercy of the Almighty. And everything grew dark before me . . . a swarm of atoms flying in from every direction clouded my sight and my mind and I heard Mansour's voice, which seemed distant to me, infinitely distant, evoking his journeys into the desert, atop his dune . . . After they listened closely to him, he was asked if it had been anything like a pilgrimage . . . to which Mansour replied that it was his Hajj, that once he arrived atop his dune he turned about within himself and around himself until he saw himself in procession around the Kaaba and in procession around the Earth and the Sun and in procession around the galaxy . . . until one of the members of the royal family stood up, so it seemed to me at the time, and interrupted him by crying out: Be quiet, unbeliever! Your words soil this hallowed ground! Then he strode over to the president of the session and whispered something to him. Then he returned, quietly, to sit down on the gold-embroidered divan. The cadi, Abou Daoud, conferred with his two coadjutors and the sentence was what it had to be and was pronounced in that same language, that same Arabic that Hallaj heard spoken during his second trial, as if shifting a thousand years backward. At the reading of the judgment, I didn't feel much of anything, apart from the sensation of falling into the infinite void that separates two atoms.

11.

WHERE HAD ALL OF IT GONE? Through which fissure had it all escaped? What winds had carried away our desires and our hopes of understanding something that was sufficiently fixed, stable, and true? When, still naive in the back of the classroom at our French high school in Damascus, so excited to discover the power of our minds, the pleasures of reasoning, we dove without restraint into the vast seas of algebra of geometry and philosophy . . . Naive and audacious, we attempted to make out the legacies and the transmissions from one civilization to another, from one thinking to another, and what joy and what delight in our discovery of the incredible resemblance between the *Treatise on Unity* by Ibn 'Arabi and Spinoza's *Ethics* . . . what delight and what joy to discover, as if by dominoes falling, across the centuries, the same intuition in Plotinus, Ibn Sina, and Bergson. Which winds, my God, which winds could have been able to carry off our souls? The naivety, the audacity, and the certainty that Abdelkader, Poincaré, and Bergson all had the same eyes . . . and the fantasy that they could have possibly made eye contact, even if it was only once. What sands, my God, could have so deeply buried our selves?

It all seemed so unreal to me, Mansour, as unreal as this esplanade and this crowd . . . I understood nothing of the words of the cadi Abou Daoud al-Qassimi, no more than I do those he speaks at this very moment, directed toward this silent and attentive crowd, which is also trying to understand the point of your martyrdom . . . or perhaps not, perhaps it had understood from the beginning, perhaps it had decided from the very beginning and all of this is really no more than a farce, no more than a dramatic performance, and everything will resume its course without leaving the slightest trace of your passage. In 922, the same sentence, word for word, must have been handed down at the trial of Mansur al-Hallaj who, the same as you, allowed himself to be led to the center of the great esplanade in Baghdad to lose his head . . . That Thursday, March 26, 922, a great crowd gathered to see Hallaj's lengthy torment, to see his limbs cut off one at a time, his head torn off and then displayed, his body burnt and his ashes scattered, on Friday, March 28, from atop a minaret, and carried by the winds that blew that day to the banks of the Tigris . . . and they spread far beyond the Tigris and its confluences and the Persian Gulf and the Arabian Sea, coming to earth in Persia, returning, so to speak, to the tortured's place of birth, and creating in this way a martyr of divine love and perhaps participating in the prosperity of the Shiite thinking that had been borne by men who devoted hours and days and years . . . entire lives to the seeking out and the understanding of all of the substance of the texts. And yet, beyond the Najd and beyond the unending Arabian desert and beyond the immense sea that separated the two peoples of a same civilization, it all came back to the same point, as if shifting a thousand years backward . . . Across the way, in a manner of speaking, in Tehran or Isfahan, maybe two guys and a young woman had lived through the same shipwreck as we had and were about to founder just like us after having clung desperately, just like us, to the texts of Suhrawardi and the thinking of al-Shirazi or Tabrizi in hopes of not leaving this world without having understood anything about it. But was it necessary, as Poincaré wrote, in order to live in this world, to know the number of ladybugs it contained . . . or did he just think this while admiring Algiers through the window of the great amphitheater and while Bergson calculated the variations of the section of a cube and while Abdelkader mathematically unwound the interlacing of the divine Umayyad Mosque . . .

We agreed, you and I, in the back of the classroom in our Damascus high school, when we sought to resolve a problem or to understand a situation, we agreed that there was a kind of continuity to ignorance. Right up until the accident. Our thoughts continually drifted in a void much in the way that Abdelkader's hand advanced perpetually in the direction of his friend's hypothetical shoulder . . . in this way free of any encounter, our ignorance flowed along the billions of circuits of our brains until an unexplained discontinuity transformed it into perfect understanding. In the back of the classroom, we were waiting, thinking and discussing and dreaming, for that discontinuity, that accident, to put us face to face with a reality until that point unknown. But where had all of it gone? Through which fissure had it all escaped? What winds had carried off our desires and our hopes of understanding anything about anything at all? We have been carried off by opposing winds and we have ended up stuck in this dusty grid until your body suffered from everything of which your self had been deprived. You found refuge among the sands and I pictured you atop your dune, following the thread of your thoughts, continuously, right up until an accident took place, right up until an unexpected leap revealed something else to you, something out of the ordinary, a moment outside of time during which you saw, perhaps, the shadow of a saber. When your executioner brings his blade down upon your offered neck and your whole is divided into parts, at which exact moment will you leave us? At which exact moment do we pass on? Between two things, but also between two states, as close together as they may be, there is always a path leading from one to the other . . . and along this path, there is inevitably an intermediary state and so on to infinity, just as sprawling as the universe that contains us. So when will you pass on, Mansour? At which exact moment? Or maybe never? A trace of you, eternally, in the infinite that separates two seconds that follow one after the other, two fractions of a second that follow one after the other, two thousandths of a second that follow one after the other . . . amid the infinite, stuck between two dust specks of an instant, you will reside in this unforeseen eye of the needle, within the infinite that conceals itself in behind . . . and I am here this morning, right near you, and I beg once again all that you can grant me as far as forgiveness and love . . . and I am here this morning before you rejoin the infinite that the blade will liberate. Take me with you, Mansour, I won't be a heavy weight to lift off this earth . . . I have so little strength left, Mansour, that you'll have no difficulty raising me up from down here. I grew lighter atop your dune, infinitely so. From that river of sand where we wandered, was it necessary to consider each grain, to have a precise understanding of each one, or instead was it necessary only to consider the whole? And when I saw you cross the crest of your dune, when you followed that line with the elegance of a tightrope walker and the grace of an angel, I could clearly see that you simultaneously considered each grain of sand and the whole that made up the dune . . . I could see Poincaré balanced on both sides, like at the summit of two ways of thinking, advancing into the yellow brilliance of the desert and addressing the void that surrounded him: *Then I turned to the study of arithmetic questions, without much apparent success, and without a suspicion that it might have anything to do with my previous research. Disgusted with my failure, I went to spend a few days at the seaside, and I thought of other things. One day, while walking atop the cliff, the idea came to me, with just the same characteristics of brevity, suddenness and immediate certainty, that the arithmetic transformations of quadratic forms were identical to those of non-Euclidian geometry.* I was sinking into the hollows in the sand and there was no one but you to lift me out. How, Mansour, did you manage to reach me? What miracle nullified the distance that separated us? Or, between you and me, between two things, between A and B, that distance is a part of the immensity of space and time that contains us . . . such an amazingly infinitesimal distance . . . that there is no longer any separation between you and me and A is inside B and the blade of the saber has never been separated from the smallest particle of your neck. I climbed up onto the highest dune and I scoured the infinite expanse with my eyes and I looked everywhere for it . . . but I did not find it. And so I sat down, I drowned in the yellow immensity and I searched within myself . . . it was there deep within me.

Gassouh! Gassouh! they shout again now that you are already on your knees, your neck extended and prepared to receive the blade that will divide you in two as if anything at all can be divisible. *Gassouh! Gassouh!* cries in a virile melee not this crowd but this black horde draped in long white clothing, shouting and pushing and impatient to see the miracle that constitutes the divisibility of a single being by two. And me, I'm there, lost among them with my gaze riveted to the sky so as to not see your torment. Eyes lost in the immensity of the sky above Al Safat Square like you Mansour atop your dune eyes lost in the immensity of the desert, in the hope of bringing an end to this unbearable worry that is comprehension. As Abdelkader had been, his eye invoking the protection of the geometric forms of the tiling, the mosaics or the ornaments of that great mosque which was in a certain way the visible beginnings of Islam and its grandeur, stuck in the squares and star-shaped polygons, stuck in the complexity of the symmetries and the rotating tessellations, stuck and slipping without cease around the circumferences of the circles, without cease without end and without exit, lost as one can lose oneself in the desert and seeking refuge for his mind, in a manner of speaking, within that superior intelligence so as to hopefully appease his soul because he could not comprehend why the tribes had abandoned him nor why the Duke of Aumale had held him prisoner so long, no more than he would understand, later on, the intense friendship of Napoléon III and France's eagerness to decorate him to photograph him to exhibit him and he also wouldn't have understood, even if he have lived as long as Noah or even as long as Abraham, the plundering of the country to which he had in a manner of speaking given birth, nor its destruction and ruin by the dark hordes who pillaged and killed in the name of Islam . . . or not . . . but the hordes of Yajuj and Majuj who poured out of the Pashtun mountains or hurled themselves from atop the cliffs of the Najd only then to hurtle down from the heights of the Atlas or the Djurdjura or the Aures and swoop down on the cities as if a single man, or even more a horrendous beast, face marked by screams and eyes full of hatred, to destroy everything and make a clean slate of everything it had been possible to build, patiently, ingeniously, intelligently, just as much to bear witness to the greatness of the divine as to bear witness to the human exception . . . to make a clean slate of the past until there was no longer any possible future. Those black hordes come out of lands just as black and resolutely determined to level anything that could proudly stand tall to make room for emptiness and likely for less than emptiness and even less than oblivion . . . those black hordes exterminating the darkness itself until the advent of the end of days or, in any case, the end of Islam.

When his heart had finally managed to contain the love of humanity in its entirety, that of the dead like that of the living, there was no longer room for anything but the love of God.

Gassouh! For the love of God, *gassouh!*

12.

THE GALLOPING GAZELLES on the vast prairies of your heart kick up too little dust, the noise of their flight as light as that of hooves on sand. But the muffled echo of their hooves propagates in circles, opening out like those of a drop of water that slams into the ocean, taken up in a wave that swells and grows until it becomes a tsunami . . . and in the same way, when your head falls on the mat that is being trampled on by the unbelievers, it will be a sound as faint as that of a hoof on sand . . . a tiny little sound, dry and imperceptible, that the years and the decades will cause to swell like a wave that swells of its own volition and that will come crashing down in a deafening roar . . . because, how could it be otherwise? How could your martyrdom be as insignificant as the extinction of a butterfly? And your ordeal as ephemeral as a caress? Yesterday, I fled the courthouse, letting loose the horses of your Camaro which carried me away far to the west, the sun in my face and the dunes in the distance. From cliff to cliff, I flew along a yellow road, covered in dust that the sun reflected without any glare . . . a fog of sand fell continually on the road, the bridges, the *wadis*, the palm groves, and the rocky faces of the Najd . . . in that dust that fell like rain, the setting sun plunged that entire backdrop into an almost greenish paleness and was no more, itself, than a pale and ordinary star vanishing behind patches of fog that blanketed the surface of a sky turned menacing. A storm rumbled behind the dunes . . . but what did the storm and its consequences matter? Behind me, Riyadh also disappeared into the fog of sand and the top of Kingdom Tower already no longer existed, as if its construction had never been completed . . . Where is all of it going? you said. And you, Mansour? Where will you go? Elsewhere? Or will you remain here? Beneath the dry earth of the Ad Deerah cemetery, across the street . . . under a rock . . . lost among the stones laid over remains that are just as insignificant as stones. Or you'll go off somewhere else even as you remain here, once the blade that your executioner is raising in front of this suddenly silent crowd arrives at the end of its long journey to reach your neck . . . in front of this crowd which will see almost nothing of your separation seeing how everything is growing whiter and whiter, more and more blurred by the winds full of dust that blow among us. Where will you go once the blade has crossed the infinite distance that separates it from you? Will you rediscover the infinite from which you are constituted? When, as Hallaj did, you hear the words *Here I am now in the dwelling place of my desires* and when you feel the iron cleave your flesh and when you accede to the dwelling place of your desires . . . You will once and forever be the point and the circumference reunited, the here and the elsewhere reunited. This saber that gleams only in the eyes of the crowd, will it only manage to travel half its path and then half of half . . . and if it should actually reach its destination, at which moment will you disappear? Between which infinities will you find sufficient oblivion for you to gather together your soul? Or maybe, for the first time in the history of humanity, this paradox will not make it all the way to its contradiction . . . and for the first time the blade of the saber will never reach the neck of its victim . . . Abdelkader reached out his arm toward Dupuch's shoulder the same way your executioner raises his saber to the sky . . . and all of Abdelkader's willpower hadn't sufficed to hold back his hand and all of my willpower, it hadn't sufficed either to keep me on that long yellow and dusty road that I hoped would never end so that we could remain there . . . eternally.

I arrived at Ksour al-Moqbel where, from the top of a minaret, the call to prayer calmly rang out. I stopped near a mosque with the desire to go in and pray for a miracle to protect us from this reality . . . but I couldn't manage to get out of the luxurious interior of what had been your beautiful red Camaro and I stayed there, listless, watching the believers rush to give thanks to the Lord of the Worlds . . . Reaching me, carried by the winds of the desert, was the imam's gentle and serene voice. Windows open and eyes closed, I listened to that prayer as if it was your final prayer. As if it was the rites that you were due . . . *And because of their saying: "We slew the Messiah, Jesus, son of Mary, Allah's messenger"* . . . *they slew him not nor crucified him, but it appeared so unto them,* شبه لهم *. . . But Allah took him up unto Himself. And Allah was ever Mighty, Wise . . .* And the night fell almost as quickly as the blow of a saber and I mingled my prayer with that of the believers, opening my eyes in the direction of your dunes, unfolding without any astonishment an unending sky, and calling out to God, from beyond the infinite that separates us, so that he listens to my prayers . . .

I will be the one to pray! I will be the invoker! Sliding down onto my knees beneath this sky full of the infinite where I will be the implorer the supplicant who opens himself up to Him to pray that He save the one who has loved him so because he no longer belongs to the ephemeral . . . he who has loved him so cannot disappear . . . You cannot kill the one who has loved you so! By opening myself up to the opening He had left above us . . . facing that unending sky . . . By opening up my voice and daring to ask Him

Let him say and become

Let him become the infinite

Let him become eternity

Let him become You

Let him love You and become You

You who speaks

You who knows

You who can

You who acts

I am on my knees so that you will lift him up . . . and I have just now implored it one more time, without holding back my voice, to the menacing looks of the still silent crowd . . . I have just now cried it out instead of reciting it as I clear myself a path toward the center from where you will rise up . . . a path like a transversal trajectory along which I was likely given kicks and spat on . . . but I am here, a few feet away from you and I am crying out your name. Mansour! Mansour! Piercing through the concentric circles that have tightened around you, crying out your name, receiving the blows of the unbeliev-ers, anointed by gobs of their spit and mouth bloodied, so that you will know one last time all of my love. I want to be in the first circle, among the next of kin, even if that proximity might reserve for me a fate similar to yours. Is there also an order where you are going? Concentric circles around the light of lights? Or is there nothing other than your light? Neither order nor disorder nor objects nor anything else at all and in a way that is just as implausible as there being anything here . . . Or maybe there is nothing but disorder and maybe things are distributed over there just as randomly as they are here where we have exactly the same odds of having different lives . . . where, you the same as me, we might never have known this kingdom of Saudi Arabia and where you just as easily could have been the opposite of Stan whom Nadine would have met in a hectic and exciting Paris, which would have brought you together for life and nothing but life . . . Or is there perhaps, like here, equal amounts of order and disorder, so that chance, perverted by the wills of certain great men, could very well have arranged everything differently in a peaceful and luminous Damascus that we had never left . . . but there was nothing but a long black rumbling, interminable, and I again hear the deafening crash of hooves that turned over our lands. The gazelles of your heart fly for the east of the East, there where the sun rises and never sets.

Night had come to blanket my mind and extinguish my voice to leave what I still had left of a soul to gallop behind the gazelles of your heart, to attempt to follow their trajectories as they diverged one from the next until my final slumber to which you came, in my dream, to say your farewells. Your hair had grown down to your feet and you had eyes that gleamed brighter than a diamond. I was once again stretched out on the sand of your desert and you had leaned over me and you smiled, telling me that it was Friday, like today, and like the day when the ashes of al-Hallaj were scattered to the four winds and the Tigris carried them away to irrigate great swaths of earth. I welcomed your visit last night the same way al-Ma'mun received that of Aristotle, in 829, enjoining him to consider as speech only speech which conforms to reason . . . I welcomed your visit the same way Muhyi al-Din, Abdelkader's father, welcomed that of his master 'Abd al-Qadir Jilani, announcing to him that his son would be sultan of the West, and responding in this way to his desire to understand by means other than reason. You had leaned over me and you took my hand in yours and you ordered me, with all your love: You will be my eyes! My eyes and my voice! and you said to me: Your mind is a great levee, built over many centuries by those who came before you, and there you must take refuge each time the waters where you swim grow cloudy and each time the lands you roam are without paths. Your mind is a great levee, and you must frequent it for as long as you will seek to know the destination of the roads traced upon the earth and each time the waves seem to want to inform you of something. Your mind is a great levee full of pitfalls on which you will stumble and you will sometimes find yourself in the mud and sometimes in the brambles but you will get up again each time. You will go to find the sense of things by diving into the sea until the waves hold you up and carry you back to your levee. You will train your eyes on virgin lands and there you will trace new roads. I welcomed your visit like an inheritance but I didn't yet know this when I awoke, inside your Camaro, in Ksour al-Moqbel, smelling of embers and ashes, and in that terrifying morning I had to live through to get myself to you. Yes, I will be your eyes, Mansour! And when my mind allows it, I will also be your voice! The billions upon billions of particles of dust fall on us like a rain of glints from mirrors reflecting one another in a brilliant light. I will be your eyes and your voice!

You are on your knees now and the crowd is fused together in silence . . . silence so as to hear the last prayer that Judge Abou Daoud has reserved for you and the sound of the blade that will cut through your neck and that, imperceptible, of the impact of your head as it falls on the much-trampled mat. This is where we are now, Mansour . . . You don't see us anymore, Mansour, but know that we are all around you. Hallaj has returned from March 26, 922 and has made his way through this impure crowd to take my hand and finish bringing me to the first circle, among those close to you, among your friends, Mansour . . . There are some here whom I recognize and still others, all dressed in white, in a tight circle around you . . . I recognize Plato and Plotinus, Suhrawardi and Ibn Sina, Abdelkader and Ibn 'Arabi . . . as for the others, those I do not recognize, their faces smile at me in this tragic moment . . . And who knows, maybe Poincaré is among them, Bergson and maybe even Louis-Napoléon . . . and who knows, Jesus, Moses, Abraham . . . All here so that before our eyes the center and the circumference be reunited, the here and the elsewhere, the visible and the hidden reunited, the rational and the irrational reunited. The winds redouble in intensity. Everything is now so white, all that remains is light on light.

Abou Daoud joins his hands together over his head and opens his mouth to initiate his prayer of farewell but nothing comes out . . . Nothing but silence in the whirling winds. Lord, grant me access to one atom of your knowledge, that which reduced mountains to dust, so that I may understand the slightest little bit of anything about this entire story. Abou Daoud turns his eyes toward your executioner who brings his sword down into the whirling winds and the silence is split asunder by the sound of a sword cutting into sand . . . and the sound of a heap of sand falling onto the mat that has been rolled out at the center of Al Safat . . . By the light of lights, I swear that an atom of your truth would make me into The Truth before its power reduces all the cliffs of the Najd to dust. Your executioner turns to the crowd and lets loose a cry that remains voiceless before the eyes of the crowd as they attempt to see you through the billions upon billions of atoms of dust that veil your miracle. Give me the strength of an atom of your truth so that I may understand that you became sand the moment the blade grazed a single atom of your skin.

It is Abdelkader, before that still-ignorant crowd, who pronounces what is meant to explain your passion and your miracle. As if his presence wasn't just as miraculous, he kneels down before the clothing that you left on that mat which should have collected your blood and your parts . . . but you are not made of parts.

I am God, I am the creature
I am the Lord, I am the servant
I am the Throne, I am the trampled mat
I am hell and I am blissful eternity
I am the water, I am the fire, I am the air and the earth
I am the number and the way
I am the presence and the absence
I am the essence and the trait
I am proximity and distance
All being is my being
I am the One
I am the Only

Abdelkader bin Muhyi al-Din
Damascus, May 26, 1883

TRANSLATOR'S ACKNOWLEDGMENTS

Special thanks to Renee Altergott, Santiago Artozqui, Heidi Denman, Mohamed Elkhadiri, Ryad Girod, Adam Levy, Lara Vergnaud, and Rawad Wehbe.

RYAD GIROD was born in 1970 in Algiers, where he teaches mathematics in the Lycée International d'Alger. Girod is a part of what the French press have labeled the October Generation, along with fellow writers such as Adlène Meddi, Samir Toumi, and others who came of age around the time of the October Riots in 1988. Winner of the Assia-Djebar Grand Prize, this is his first book to appear in English.

CHRIS CLARKE was born in Western Canada and currently lives in Philadelphia, PA. His previous translations include work by Raymond Queneau, Pierre Mac Orlan, and François Caradec. He was awarded the 2019 French-American Foundation Translation Prize for fiction in 2019 for his translation of Marcel Schwob's *Imaginary Lives* (Wakefield Press), a prize for which he was a finalist in 2017 for his translation of Nobel Prize-winner Patrick Modiano's *In the Café of Lost Youth* (NYRB Classics). He is a PhD Candidate in French at The Graduate Center (CUNY), and his dissertation examines the role of translation in the career of French author Raymond Queneau.

Transit Books is a nonprofit publisher of international and American literature, based in Oakland, California. Founded in 2015, Transit Books is committed to the discovery and promotion of enduring works that carry readers across borders and communities. Visit us online to learn more about our forthcoming titles, events, and opportunities to support our mission.

TRANSITBOOKS.ORG